SMALL ROBOT
BIG ADVENTURE

HODDER CHILDREN'S BOOKS

First published in Great Britain in 2019 by Hodder and Stoughton

1 3 5 7 9 10 8 6 4 2

Text copyright © Shane Hegarty, 2019
Illustrations copyright © Ben Mantle, 2019

A CIP catalogue record for this book
is available from the British Library.

ISBN 978 1 44494 936 0

Printed and bound in Great Britain by
CPI Group (UK) Ltd, Croydon, CR0 4YY

The paper and board used in this book
are made from wood from responsible sources.

MIX
Paper from
responsible sources
FSC® C104740

Hodder Children's Books
An imprint of
Hachette Children's Group
Part of Hodder and Stoughton
Carmelite House
50 Victoria Embankment
London EC4Y 0DZ

An Hachette UK Company
www.hachette.co.uk

www.hachettechildrens.co.uk

BOOT

SMALL ROBOT
BIG ADVENTURE

SHANE HEGARTY

ILLUSTRATED BY BEN MANTLE

For Caoimhe.
You are a wonderful
daughter and a
fantastic editor.

THE ⚙NLY THINGS
I REMEMBER

I woke up with only two-and-a-half memories.

Something was very wrong. I should have remembered so much more. My head is built to hold millions of memories, and I also have extra space in my left butt-cheek, in case of emergencies.

The first memory is fifteen seconds long. A young girl pulls wrapping paper away from my face. She shrieks happily and her eyes twinkle brightly. The girl has dark hair tied up in a bun and a smile so wide it almost reaches her ears.

Dangling from the girl's neck is a butterfly pendant with sixteen tiny green, red, yellow and blue jewels dazzling in its wings.

This girl is the very first person I remember seeing.

"A toy robot! Thank you, Grandma!" the girl screams in delight.

Behind her is a smiling woman with white hair, standing beside balloons that read 'Happy 7th Birthday!' She must be 'Grandma'.

"I thought, what better present for my cute, cuddly Beth than a cute, cuddly robot," says Grandma.

That's how I know the girl's name is Beth.

"Thankyouthankyouthankyouthankyou thankyou!" says Beth.

I see my reflection in a mirror. I am a little shorter than Beth. My body is silver-green and shaped like a light bulb, with my belly round and tough, yet still soft to touch or hug. I waggle the four chunky fingers on my hands. I do not waggle my toes because I don't have toes, just egg-shaped legs.

"Oh, look at its face!" says Beth. "I love it!"

My head is a wide oval, with a smooth screen

curving along the front of it. On the screen, tiny dots of colourful light flow together and make a cartoon human face.

When I imagine myself smiling, bright blue eyes and a warm orange smile appear on the screen.

Beth and her grandma laugh and laugh and laugh and—

That memory ends.

The second memory is shorter than the first, only seven seconds long. Beth is in this one too, but she's quite a bit taller than me now, and her hair a little longer. Again she wears the butterfly pendant, but this time one of the jewels has been lost from a wing. It means this memory must take place later than the first.

She is giggling at me because, for some reason, I am wearing a flowerpot as a hat – with the flowers still in it. I also have a multicoloured hula-hoop around my waist and a purple dog-shaped balloon rising from a string tied to one of my fingers.

Beth is laughing so hard I wonder if she will burst.

Thankfully, Beth doesn't burst. She just keeps laughing until this memory ends.

Then there is the last memory. The half-memory.

This one doesn't work properly. It's glitchy and jumpy and lasts just 5.824 seconds.

Beth is much taller than before. Her face looks older. A lot of time must have passed since the memory where I had a flowerpot as a hat.

She's not laughing.

But she still wears the butterfly pendant around her neck. I can see it poking out from the collar of her heavy grey coat.

We are outside on a street. There's a large sign on the wall behind Beth – an orange circle with a white, sideways triangle inside it.

I can hear water rushing loudly somewhere nearby.

GLITZCH. JUMP. Beth bends down to me. Tears are pooling in her eyes.

PHITTZP. JUMP. Weak daylight glints off the butterfly pendant. There are three tiny hollows where the jewels have fallen out. Only thirteen left.

SF|PZ. JU̱MP. Beth says one word,"… love …"

The memory freezes.

And I remember nothing else. Maybe I was switched off. Maybe I stopped working properly.

I don't know how long I was like this for. All I know is that when I turned back on again, I said one word, "Boot."

And I found myself rolling and tumbling in a great wave of rubbish towards the smashing jaws of a massive, metal-munching grinding machine.

B✸✸T

A car licence plate struck me on the forehead with a *ting*.

A large tractor tyre smashed down a centimetre in front of my face, almost taking off my head. It bounced onwards, exploding as it was bitten by the grinder's huge, metal teeth.

I was fifteen metres away and sliding fast. I knew danger when I saw it. That's because I actually saw the word DANGER flashing in my vision – big red letters and a high-pitched alarm, warning me I could lose my head to the falling rubbish.

I didn't want to lose my head. I would have been able to replace an arm, perhaps. Or my right butt-cheek. But *not* my head.

DANGER.

Ten metres to the grinder, which was turning even the thickest chunks of steel into metal crumbs.

I was a robot. I knew I should use my sophisticated computer brain to assess the situation, calculate an escape route and put my plan into action without delay.

But I didn't. Instead I flapped my arms about while bumping and rolling down the slope, unable to find a grip on the ground.

Why did I do this? Is this what you humans call 'panic'?

I didn't like it.

DANGER DANGER.

A falling toaster hit my body.

The drawer in my left hip popped open and something sparkly fell out and away, snagging itself on the edge of a cracked plastic play kitchen that was sliding down the slope beside me.

It was Beth's butterfly pendant! Its little jewels glinted, their colours bright against the grime of the rubbish. There were only twelve jewels in it now.

DANGER DANGER DANGER.

Only five metres to the grinder, and destruction.

Beth had lost her butterfly pendant, I realised.

She had lost me.

"… love …" she had said in my memory. I didn't know how or why, but I was certain that word was very powerful for humans.

Seeing the pendant and thinking of Beth must have activated my cool, calm programming again, because I suddenly knew what to do.

I had to escape. I had to return the pendant to Beth. Bring *myself* home to her.

DANGER DANGER DANGER DANGER.

A long metal spike tumbled high through the

air, stabbing itself into the bare dirt ground at the mouth of the grinder.

I had one chance at escape. I calculated the angle, the speed of the fall and – most importantly – how much it would matter to Beth if I saved her pendant.

Leaping towards the spike, I hooked my fingers around it and swung around to grab the pendant, just before the play kitchen was eaten up with a horrible,

splintering **CRACK**.

I'd made it! But I was not safe yet.

I put the pendant back in my drawer and slammed it shut, then scanned the rest of the rubbish tumbling into the grinder. I spotted another metal pole, one that humans use for skiing. I leaned down and grabbed it just in time, then stuck it into a smudge of soft ground further above me.

Sticking the spike and the pole, one at a time, into the ground, I slowly worked my way back up the slope, through the avalanche of rubbish.

A hurtling suitcase clipped my shoulder and I almost slid down again, but I tightened my grip and managed to keep pulling up the slope until the horrible noise grew quieter and the ground was becoming flat again.

Nearing the top of the slope, I saw the back of a truck open and release another load of rubbish.

I clung on tight while this new wave of debris rolled towards the grinder.

A football bounced over me. A filthy doll flopped by. A rusty tricycle wheeled down the slope as if it was being ridden by an invisible child.

I held on until everything passed and DANGER stopped flashing in my vision. The high-pitched alarm in my head ceased. It was now so quiet I could hear the whirring of my brain as it tried to figure out why I was here and what I should do now.

The truck was rumbling away from me down the road. I wondered if it was driven by a human. Because of Beth and her grandma, I knew humans were good. If I could find one, they'd realise I'd been tipped into the grinder by mistake and would help me find Beth.

I followed the truck.

In the breeze, loose items trickled from the mounds of waste that towered either side of the road. A round mirror rolled across the ground and spun to a stop in front of me.

I stood over it. My silver-green body was grubby, and there were smears of dirt across the curved screen that made up my face. I wiped it clean and revealed a thin crack down the part of my screen that you humans would call your cheek. In my memories, I saw no crack and I didn't know how it had got there.

My orange smile turned blue and upside down.

All I *did* know was that I only had two-and-a-half memories, I was lost, and one word kept going around and around in my brain.

Boot.

Boot.

"Boot," I said to a rat that was chewing through some loose wires in the fallen rubbish.

The rat didn't answer me.

"Boot," I said again, louder this time.

Boot.

Then I realised what it must mean – why it was the first word I said aloud.

'Boot' was my name.

I AM N⚙T A BISCUIT

At the end of the road, beside where the truck had parked, I could see a hut. A pair of muddy shoes sat on its doorstep. Someone must be inside.

I swivelled my body towards the hut. I whistled a happy tune as I walked.

Confused, I stopped. I hadn't meant to whistle a happy tune.

I walked again. I whistled again. Worse, I skipped and clicked my heels together.

Something was wrong with me. My body was doing things I wasn't telling it to do. I had to concentrate hard just to walk without whistling or clicking my heels together.

Nearing the hut, I asked myself some questions.

Why did I remember almost nothing about my life?

How could I find Beth using just two-and-a-half memories?

And when I was falling into the grinder, why had I panicked like a human when I should have been calm and calculated like a robot?

I knew I was a robot, just like I knew the rat was a rat. And the tyre was a tyre. All that information was in my head, put there before I had arrived at Beth's home.

It's the same way you humans just *know* you are humans. At least, I think that's how it is. Maybe I'm wrong. Maybe you sometimes wake up in the morning and leap from your bed, shocked to discover you're not a chocolate biscuit.

I climbed the steps to the hut, drew an orange smile on my face and stretched to reach the handle. I swung in through the door, ready to say a big, friendly 'hello' to whoever was inside.

"Pineapples!" I announced.

I did *not* mean to say pineapples.

A man sitting behind a desk inside the hut got such a fright he toppled backwards off his chair with a **THUD**.

The hut was filled with pieces of electronics –
old and broken radios, televisions, fans – piled so
high that they blocked most of the light coming
in from the small window.

An upside-down drone was on the desk,
a faded skull and crossbones printed on its
underside, wires exposed and propellers put
aside, like it was being fixed.

The rest of the desk was covered in old
crumpled food containers and soft-drinks cans. A
half-eaten burger sat in its wrapping.

The man squashed the burger with his palm
as he grabbed the desk to help himself up. He
had wiry white hair under a lopsided baseball cap
with *Krush 'em Kwik* emblazoned across it. His
grey stubble was patchy, his nose red, and his skin
looked as worn out as the paint peeling off the
walls of his old hut.

On his grubby boilersuit, a faded badge read
HI, MY NAME IS FLINT.

Flint looked a bit broken, just like me.

I wanted to say sorry, to tell him I was lost and ask how I had ended up here, but my words were all mixed up.

"Freckles! I am so freckles," I said instead.

He glared at me, with one eye more open than the other. He was missing two teeth and had chipped three more. Half-chewed burger meat was lodged inside one cheek.

"You crazy little bag of bolts, how did you get in here?" Flint scowled, wiping burger mush across his uniform. "Did you escape the grinder?"

Flint did not look friendly and he was talking about me like I was just another piece of rubbish. But I was not rubbish and I was sure Flint would understand there had been a mistake if I explained everything to him, so I tried to say, "I need help."

Instead, I said, "I weed kittens."

It was no use. I couldn't make my voice say the words my brain wanted it to.

Maybe I could *show* Flint my problem instead. I drew a cartoon butterfly on my screen and made it flutter across my face, then opened the drawer at my waist to show Flint the pendant. He pushed my hand away before I could take it out.

"I don't have time to talk to a walking toaster," he said, one eye opening wider while the other one narrowed, like he was trying to see inside my circuits. "Almost all my pals have lost their jobs to robots, and if I let a little blob of rust like you walk away from this scrapyard then my boss will finally find an excuse to replace me too. That ain't gonna happen."

He was not a happy human. He was an angry human. I guessed this because his teeth were clenched and his voice was getting louder, while his finger jabbed at me.

"Thirty-three years I've been at *Krush 'em*

Kwik and tearing robots apart is my favourite bit of the job," he said.

I felt like someone was twisting every wire in my tummy. This must be what it feels like to be scared.

Why was I having these feelings at all? I was a robot. Robots aren't supposed to feel.

But I didn't have time to think about this now.

Flint walked towards me, forcing me to reverse and bump against a table. A microwave crashed to the floor.

In among the piles of electronics were other things. Robot arms. Robot legs. Robot *heads*. Flint must have been taking robots apart like he was doing with that drone on his desk.

My face shook. That must be the fear again. I wanted to be cool and calm and more like the robot I was supposed to be, but I didn't know how to stop the fear from showing.

"You're just a machine, so stop trying to make

me feel sorry for you," said Flint, picking up a baseball bat and tapping the wall beside my head menacingly. **DANGER** flashed in my vision again.

"I am cakes – underpants – *lost*," I finally said, dodging under Flint's baseball bat and looking towards the open door out of the hut.

"You'd better believe you're lost. Now stand still while I make sure you don't get found again," said Flint, jabbing at me with the bat.

Without even knowing I could do it, I dropped to the floor, curled into a ball and rolled away. I bashed against the broken electronics, causing a tower of televisions to crash down between me and Flint.

I kept rolling all the way out the door and across the gravel, picking up speed.

"Come back!" I heard Flint shout as he tried to push aside the pile of TVs. "I'm ordering you!"

I knew I was meant to do what humans told me to, but the feeling of fear was buzzing so strongly through my wires, it was like *that* was in charge of me now.

Flint kept yelling stop, but every part of me – every circuit, every screw – said I was not safe yet. I just rolled and rolled until I rolled into the scrapyard's fence. I popped my head up and saw a small gap in the chains.

So I curled up again and rolled through that.

"When I catch you again, I'll tear you into strips of metal spaghetti!" I heard Flint shout from the hut, still trapped inside.

Many thoughts were whizzing through my head. Why was this man being so horrible? Maybe he was angry because he was sad? Did he not have a robot friend when *he* was a boy?

Seventy-three seconds passed before DANGER stopped flashing in my vision. I calculated that it would be safe to unfurl now and see exactly where I had ended up.

I was on a wide and quiet road leading away from the scrapyard. I started running into the unknown, as fast as I could. Even though I was very, very scared, I was still whistling that happy tune as I ran.

I didn't know where I was running to. I just knew I had to find my way to somewhere safe.

I had to find a way home to Beth.

SITUATI●N: TERRIBLE

You humans have no idea how easy it is for you
to run.

You've got legs and heads and spines that have
evolved over millions of years to help you walk
and jog easily. Except for toddlers, of course.
They are always falling. Sideways. Forwards.
Backwards. On their bottoms. Head over heels.
All those things at the same time. Toddlers look
silly. Even a robot can see that.

Running is *not* so easy for me. I wobble when
I stride, jiggle when I sprint, topple when I trot.
I could just curl up in a ball and roll all the time,
but I can't see where I'm going.

I kept running from the scrapyard at the fastest
speed I could, which, given the slight upward

slope of the path, was 5.2 miles per hour. I made good progress until I tripped on a loose stone, fell over and landed in a patch of weeds.

Red circles appeared on my cheeks, even though I hadn't told my brain to draw them. And though the temperature of my insides was the exact same as it had always been, I felt strangely warm all of a sudden.

Was I embarrassed? Robots should not feel embarrassed.

A pigeon had settled on my head. I pushed the pigeon away and stared back down the long road behind me. Thankfully I couldn't see Flint from *Krush 'em Kwik* chasing after me. Perhaps he was just happy I was gone from his scrapyard.

I used my incredible brainpower to calculate my situation.

But the only result my incredible brainpower came up with was this: my situation was TERRIBLE.

The wide road I was on rose up ahead, into a long hill. Large, low buildings lined either side. My in-built encyclopaedia told me they were factories, but old ones with smashed windows and boarded-up doors.

Among the high weeds surrounding me sat the large metal shell of an old, burnt-out car.

Its wheels were gone and its insides were charred and blackened. I felt sad for the car, even though I knew it couldn't have felt anything at all. But *I* felt things now, so maybe it had too?

Flint had treated me like I was just a ruined old car – no use to anyone any more. But I was more than that. Beth loved me and would be missing me. Maybe this car had an owner hoping to find it, just like Beth would be wanting to find me.

These feelings made my circuits tingle strangely. I was programmed to understand and recognise feelings when I saw them in humans, but actually *feeling* them too was new to me.

Things weren't making sense. My legs felt like jelly, even though I could see they were not made of jelly at all. My brain felt fuzzy, because the feelings were getting in the way of my ability to solve problems and think clearly. I wished I could find a switch in my brain to turn the feelings off while I figured it all out.

I hid behind the wrecked car to check if any new memories had surfaced, ones that might help me understand how I'd got here, but I still only had the same two-and-a-half-memories of Beth. I recalled them again.

They were so clear that when I remembered them, it was as if I wasn't on this street but actually with her.

In the first memory, I could see the scraps of wrapping paper torn and scattered around me. I saw Beth and Grandma, and their beaming smiles. I heard her excited *Thankyouthankyouthankyouthankyouthankyou.* I saw my reflection in the mirror. The gems of her butterfly pendant glinting in the light.

In the second memory, I could see the tendrils of roots drooping over my eyes from the flowers balancing on my head. I saw the fraying strands of string tying the balloon to my finger. On the butterfly pendant, I could see the gap where a gem had come free. I could hear Beth's loud, gasping laugh.

As I watched this memory back, a strange thing happened. I let out a burst of high, giddy laughter too, like I'd burped up happiness.

That was a strange feeling that made me feel warm again. But a nice warmth, not like when I was embarrassed.

Then there was the final, messy, half-memory.

Between the glitches and jumps and gaps in this memory, some details were still clear. I had been outdoors, on a street. There was the sound of water nearby, even though I couldn't see it. There was the sign on the wall – an orange circle with a white triangle inside it. The pendant now had three jewels missing. Beth's eyes were deep brown, and wet with tears.

Why was Beth crying? I didn't know.

Then Beth said the word "… love …"

I still didn't remember a single thing after this.

I *had* to find Beth, return the butterfly pendant, make her laugh again.

The sign with the triangle was an important clue. Find that and I would find Beth.

It should be easy to see the sign somewhere in these wide streets. I moved on, my circuits less tingly, stronger even. When I thought of Beth, it felt like nothing would stop me finding her. I was … determined! Yes, determined.

I liked this feeling much more than being scared.

Then I reached the crest of the hill. A vast city of skyscrapers stretched out before me.

My search for the sign suddenly felt impossible.

My hopes of seeing Beth felt so distant.

My legs felt like jelly again.

THE CITY

It took me hours to walk to the heart of the city. Three hours and twenty-eight minutes, to be exact – yet somehow, it felt *longer*.

With every step, it was as if the buildings grew taller, the streets narrower, the shadows darker and the world so much busier, until the city became a river of sound and action, ready to sweep a small robot like myself away.

I heard the shouts of street vendors, the growl of buses, the clink of busy cafés, the clack of footsteps. And I saw people moving quickly, in every direction. Some walked. Some sat in cars that drove themselves.

"Woah, watch out," said a man, almost bumping into me as he ran by in shorts and a

T-shirt. I wondered if he was being chased by someone who might want to crush him in a grinder.

But then a woman ran by in the other direction, also in shorts and a T-shirt, and I realised they were just running because they liked running. Why would anyone *like* running? All that wobbling. And jiggling.

But there was one thing above all else that made my eyes widen with wonder.

There were robots *everywhere*.

Flying drones zipped through the air, darting in and out of tall windows to deliver and collect boxes that hung below their bellies.

Wide barrel-shaped robots rolled along the pavements, carrying heavier items, while expertly avoiding the legs of the humans walking in each direction.

I saw tall robots – some with four, or even eight, arms. They were doing lots of different jobs: washing windows, guarding offices, carrying shopping bags, directing traffic, working behind shop counters.

I watched a robot waiter serve drinks to people at one table while it wiped another table clean and then used its spare hands to light candles.

I watched a robot walking a dog, not complaining when the dog peed on its leg.

There was one type of robot that a lot of

people had. Three times my height, these robots had sleek, black, rectangular bodies and walked quite perfectly, with gently swinging arms. They didn't look like they would fall over in a patch of weeds or like a pigeon would ever bother them.

Their heads were perfectly round, with a ball-shaped screen. Messages, maps, emojis and pictures constantly flashed across them, the information always turned towards their owners.

The humans couldn't get enough of this information. To me it seemed that most were far more interested in talking to their robots than to any other people. In fact, they were so wrapped up in this information that the humans kept almost walking into each other. Only a gentle tug or nudge by their robots, who seemed to know where they were going without having to look, kept them from wandering into traffic or tripping over peeing dogs.

"Why has Dave not liked my rabbit picture yet?" one woman demanded of her robot as they passed me. "I liked his stupid picture of a squirrel yesterday."

A man and his robot passed in the opposite direction. A picture of a cat asleep on a toilet flashed on his robot's face. "Your friend Emma has posted a new picture," said the robot in a flat voice.

"That's so stupid," the man sneered. "Tell her I *love* it."

A thought occurred to me. I saw all these types of robots, yet not one of them was like me.

Maybe I was special, made just for Beth?

It wasn't just that they didn't look like me. It was that the robots just seemed, well … like robots. I knew I was a robot, but I still felt like me. They did not look like they felt *any* emotions. Any happiness, fear, panic, embarrassment, determination, anything at all.

Among all this clatter of street noise, I heard a pig's *oink*. Then a cat's *miaow*, followed by the happy *ruff* of a dog.

I saw a woman walking through the crowds, holding a long stiff lead, at the end of which were three collars attached to a robot dog, a robot cat and a robot pot-bellied pig. These were perfectly-made electronic animals, their legs making a little electronic *bizzt* as they bounced along. Their eyes flashed from deep blue to emerald green.

The woman stopped, tilted her head up and

commanded the robot pets, "Sit."

The robot pets sat.

"Roll over." They rolled over.

"Do a somersault." The dog, cat and pot-bellied pig each performed an impressive somersault and gave a little electronic *ruff, miaow* and *oink*.

The woman clapped her hands in delight, crouched and gave each of the robot animals a pat on the head.

She didn't look broken and angry like Flint, but friendly, like Beth's grandma. She seemed to care for her robots. I wondered if I should ask her for help.

The woman looked up and put a hand out. A large grey cloud had filled the slice of sky above the tall buildings. Fat drops of rain began to fall.

Just as she had done, I put my hand out and let the rain bounce off my hand. As it fell heavier, the rain started to run down my arm, dribble on to my body and clean away the dust and dirt of the scrapyard, revealing the shininess of my body.

The woman hurriedly took an umbrella from her bag and sprung it open. But she used it to protect her pets from the rain, not herself.

I wondered what would happen if I stayed in the rain. Was I waterproof? Would I rust? Would the rain creep in through the crack in my face and fill my insides with water?

I drew a little wave on my screen and let it wash away my cartoon face. I did not want that to happen. I did *not* want to get back to Beth with water sloshing between my ears.

The woman pulled up a hood on her jacket and began to walk on again.

I had to take my chance before it was too late. I stepped out in front of her.

She stopped, confused.

Through the *thump-thump* of rain, I displayed big puppy-dog eyes, wider even than those of the pretend puppy dog she had with her now.

I tried to say *hello* and instead said, "Peanuts!"

The woman's pink-painted smile broadened.

"Are you a lost robot?" she asked.

I nodded enthusiastically, causing water to pour off my head. I put my hand over the crack in my face to stop rain leaking in.

"Oh, you are delightful!" she gasped, and with her free hand, ushered me under the umbrella where I squeezed between her robot pets.

"Let's get you out of this rain before you get washed away," said the woman.

She put a spare collar around me and clipped it to the pig.

The pig snorted a high-pitched and perky snort.

I started to whistle, even though I didn't want to.

"Wonderful!" exclaimed the woman. "Let's get you home."

A PAL FOR MR PIGGLES

In the steady rain, I splashed and waddled around the puddles, trying to stay as dry as possible while being dragged between three pretend animals.

None of the pretend animals appeared bothered by the rain or, in fact, by anything at all. They had sparkling eyes, but – how can I describe this? – there was no *life* behind them. They looked as if they would have been as happy being fed into a crunching grinder as they were making their owner laugh.

Was I like this once too? A little shudder ran through my body at the thought, shaking raindrops from the surface.

Finally we reached a doorway into a building

where a rather thin, grey robot with a peaked cap on its head opened the door and the woman ushered us inside, into a wide lobby. She shook her umbrella dry behind her and handed it to the lobby robot.

"Walk on," she said, and the pets trotted across the floor, with me being dragged by the pig.

We stepped into a lift, and as the doors closed behind her, the woman bent down to me. "Oh, look at you, all shiny and with that squidgy belly. And those dents on you will buff right out."

I put my hand on my crack again, and she did the strangest thing. She spat on a tissue and used it to rub a smudge of dirt off my head.

The lift went *ping*, the doors opened and the pets trotted out and stopped by a door across the hallway, waiting patiently.

With a rattle of keys, the woman opened the door.

"Go," she said, releasing the lead so the three robots could bound inside. They pulled me after them and settled into a large basket.

I looked at the pig. It licked me with its plastic tongue.

My internal temperature was exactly the same as it ever had been, but *again* I felt a strange heat in my cheeks, just like I had when I had tripped over and fallen in the patch of weeds.

Yes, this was embarrassment all right. I was beginning to recognise it all too clearly.

"Oh, Mr Piggles must really like you," she said to me. "You two will be great pals. And I'm sure Lord Woofsalot and Countess Whiskers will like you just as much."

I looked at the dog and cat robot. They didn't look back at me.

The woman leaned down and tickled the pig under its chin. I wished I could speak in a normal way so I could explain to the woman why I needed help. I didn't want her to think I was broken, in case I was sent back to the scrapyard.

She lifted me from the basket and held me up to get a better look. I drew a smile across my face. I wanted her to like me so she would fix me. I wanted her to make my words work again, so I could tell her everything about Beth and Grandma and the pendant and—

"FRANK!" the woman shouted, so loudly it made my head rattle. "COME HERE, FRANK!"

A boy sloped into the room, a sneer on his face and a small black screen in his hand, which he did not take his eyes off. It was some sort of game, and his thumbs moved so quickly on it, I wondered for a moment if he might be a robot boy. But he had some greenish liquid running from his nose, which meant he was definitely human.

"Frank, look what I found for you," said the woman, swinging me around to show me off.

"Uh-huh," said Frank, not looking up from the game.

His mother grabbed the game away, much to Frank's horror. Then she shoved me at him. I caught sight of explosions and shooting on the screen.

"Ah, Mum!" protested Frank. "I'm nearly at level four thousand!"

"I got you a pet," said his mother.

A pet? I thought, horrified. These three animal robots might have been pets, but I was me! I was Boot.

"A pet?" said Frank. "That's not a pet. It's a cracked tin can."

The smile fell from my face. A scowl went up instead.

"It's a grumpy tin can too," said Frank, pushing past me and resuming his game.

"Now," she said, ignoring his whining, "you need a distraction from that thing in your hand and, well, you know I don't like you messing with *my* pets …"

She looked over at Countess Whiskers, Sir Woofsalot and Mr Piggles, who were each standing to attention with their heads up.

"… especially since you sat on poor Mr Piggles and broke his snout."

Mr Piggles waggled his snout. It rattled.

"But this sweet little toy robot came along, with no owner, and I thought it would make a perfect pet for you."

She held me up again. I did not like being waved about like this.

Frank had his arms crossed and his chin in his chest and looked very unimpressed. I drew the same look on my face. I was not impressed either.

"So?" said Frank, shrugging.

"So, it doesn't look like much now," said his mother, "but if you glue a horn on its face, it could be your own pet rhinoceros."

Pet rhinoceros?!

"Or we could glue big ears to it and make it your own little chimp."

"I could call it Mr Chimples," mumbled Frank, coming around to the idea. "If I make that robot my pet, can I play the game again?"

"Yes," said his mother, handing me over.

Frank stared at me, like I didn't matter. He might as well have been staring at an empty box. "Maybe I could turn this robot into my own pet leprechaun."

I searched my brain for some information on leprechauns, and when I found it I couldn't help but draw a little, red-bearded fellow on my face.

"I'll glue some old red carpet to its chin to make a beard, and put a small green hat on its head, and …"

Frank went on for a while about this, shaking me around, turning me upside down, examining me, pulling a bit on my arm.

Eventually, he threw me roughly back into the basket alongside the cat, dog and pig.

Mr Piggles licked me again.

Frank and his mother left for another room to get the old red carpet to glue to my face.

I was *not* going back to Beth dressed as a leprechaun.

The window was open a little, and outside was a metal platform and a ladder. Did I dare escape again?

"We could a glue a little pipe to its face too!" I heard Frank say in the other room.

I *did* dare escape.

I gave one last look at the empty-headed

Mr Piggles, Sir Woofsalot and Countess Whiskers. I waved goodbye, climbed out the open window and was away.

A V⚙ICE FROM AB⚙VE

I was back in the city streets, this time moving through alleyways and trying to be much more careful about who I talked to next. I was learning that just because a human looks nice on the outside, doesn't mean they will be friendly on the inside.

For a long while, I just waited behind a large bin, watching the street. But when a girl across the road dropped a drinks can on the ground, my bin grew legs and arms and walked over to pick the can up.

I was on my own and I still needed help. I decided that, even though none of them seemed to think like me, it might be safer to ask another robot.

So, carefully edging back out on to the busy street, I approached a grey robot walking a dog – a *real* dog that had stopped to sniff a lamppost.

I needed to say my words properly. I concentrated very hard. *Excuse me,* I wanted to say to the robot.

"Squeeze melons," I said instead.

Oh, those stupid words!

The robot ignored me anyway. The dog cocked a leg to pee on me. I stepped back just in time to avoid being splashed. I didn't want to get home to Beth smelling of dog pee.

Or smelling of any type of pee at all.

I moved on to a tall, sleek robot holding shopping bags outside a store. I concentrated again, ordering my brain to keep it simple and say only one word.

"Hello," I said, relieved to have finally found the right word.

The robot pulled the shopping bags closer against its sides, tightening its fingers around the handles.

"I …" I said, concentrating hard, "need … to … find my … sausages … marmalade … *owner*."

Yellow eyes flashed on the round black screen of the robot's face. "Step aside or I shall call security," it ordered sternly.

I drew a bright orange smile on my screen to show I was friendly.

"Security! Security!" the robot shouted.

Hearing a siren inside the store, I ran away. A human security guard appeared at the door behind me, his cap flashing red and blue and making a loud *whee-whoo* noise.

I hid around the corner in another alley,

grateful that the security guard didn't follow me and send me back to the scrapyard.

I wandered the alleys again, avoiding both humans and robots now. I was confused. I knew I was a robot and that I could make many calculations at super speeds, and yet every time I calculated a plan, it didn't work.

And without a plan – or help – how would I possibly find the round orange sign with the sideways triangle in it? How would I ever find Beth in this huge city?

It was while hiding in a dark alley that ran between two brick buildings that I heard an echoing clatter of metal, and a gravelly, electronic voice call out a single word,

"HELP!"

I peered into the shadows. Beneath a row of windows that ran up the side of a tall building, a small, furry creature hopped creakily on its back legs, looking up at a row of windows opposite. Moving closer, I saw it was a tattered robot dog with patchy fur, one of its eyes missing and its tongue hanging out of the side of its mouth like it might fall out at any moment.

"RUFF," said the robot dog at something in the windows, then glitched like its bark was stuck. "RUPPPPZZZZTTTTT."

I followed its one eye to where it was looking. "HELP!" I heard again, coming from somewhere above. "HELP ME, POOCHY! I'M TRAPPED!"

And then I saw it. The bottom of a scuffed robot made of hard rubber, with rectangular legs and feet, was sticking out of a window three storeys up.

"Come on, you malfunctioning mutt!" it called to the dog. "Climb up."

Poochy didn't help. It just ran around in circles, chasing its own floppy tongue.

The stuck robot needed my help. And if I helped it, then it would surely help me in return, wouldn't it?

"Squishy!" I called up to the trapped robot. "Fluffy rainbows!"

The wrong words again!

The end of a fire-escape ladder rested just on the ground where I stood. It ran up along the edge of the windows. This must have been how the robot got up there in the first place.

Carefully, I climbed the ladder, trying not to look down as I rose higher and higher and higher, until I reached the window where the robot was stuck.

From inside the window, it turned its rectangular head towards me, squeaking its blocky eyebrows together in a frown. "Who are you?" the robot asked.

I didn't know what words would come out of me, so instead, I gently wedged open the window.

Suddenly freed from the window, the robot
dropped into thin air and plunged to the
concrete below.

N✲KE

I looked down, expecting to see an explosion
of circuits and broken parts as the robot hit the
ground.

Instead, with a surprisingly boingy, rubbery
sound, the robot bounced, rolled, bounced again,
tried to stand up, fell, rolled over, walloped
against the wall and finally landed on its
rectangular feet.

"Indestructible!" it said, looking up at me. The robot had small black eyes set back in deep sockets. It had chunky but flexible lips that moved around when it spoke. And its small, rectangular right ear was hanging off.

I made my way back down the ladder, feeling a little clumsy. When I arrived at the ground, I saw that the top of my head only reached the robot's chin.

"My name is Noke," said the robot, ramming its ear back into place. "Thanks for getting me out of a jam there."

I wanted to say my name. "I am … Ploppy … Unicorns," I said. "I mean … Buckets! Oh, my words are *very* pyjamas."

Noke looked at me carefully, eyebrows meeting with a rusty squeak. "I bet I can fix your word problem."

I nodded, pleased.

Noke lurched forward, grabbed my head

firmly and thrust a finger in my ear.

"Let go of my elephants!" I protested. "Sponge away from my daffodils!"

With a swivel of its finger, Noke clicked something in my brain.

"That was not nice," I complained, then realised I could talk properly again. "Oh, you fixed me. Thank you. My name is Boot."

My face beamed a bright sunny smile.

"RUFF. RUUUPPPPSSTTTFFTT," said Poochy, wagging its rusty tail.

"How did you fix me?" I asked.

"I've been on these streets for a long time and picked up a few tricks here and there," said Noke. "You're a toy, right? You're a bit squidgy, yet tough enough to be thrown about. You have that cartoon face and a kid's voice. Am I right …?"

Without planning to, I announced, **"I am Robot-O-Fun, your Favourite Funtime Pal."**

"Well, I owe you one, Funtime," said Noke. "Anything else I can fix for you?"

"I whistle when I don't want to," I said. "And I click my heels at the wrong moments."

Noke grabbed my head again and twisted a finger in my other earhole. But something went wrong because I started to dance wildly. My arms flapped like a bird. My legs kicked up and down and sideways. I did the splits.

"What's happening?" I asked.

I leaped in the air, did a kung-fu kick against the wall, spun and landed with my arms outstretched. "Ta-dah!"

I did *not* want to say 'ta-dah'. The cheeks on my screen went red. I had that strange, hot feeling again.

"Sorry, I turned my finger the wrong way," said Noke, lurching forward as I spun past. Another twist in my earhole stopped the dance.

"Thank you," I said. Already, I could tell that Noke was different like me – or, at least, different from the other dead-eyed robots I'd met in the city.

"I'd love it if I could fix Poochy as easily," said Noke, "but the mechanical mutt has got a bit rusty over the years. Watch this. *Sit, Poochy.*"

Poochy did a backward somersault and landed on its head.

"See?" said Noke.

"Anyway, can you show me your backside?"

I was confused and my wavy mouth showed it.

Noke peered around me, before declaring, "Ah, that's no use to me. I hoped you'd have a charging port back there like me, and might have a charger on you, but you must get your energy from solar panels behind your face. Not me. I'm stuck with one of these useless old things ..."

With a waggle, a flap opened on Noke's side. Behind the flap was a big round hole – a socket for an old-fashioned power charger, the kind that hasn't been made for years. On Noke's right hand was a battery icon saying that fifty-six per cent power was left.

"If I don't get a charger soon, my battery will run out and I'll stop working. I'll be left with about as much personality as a traffic cone. And those guys are *boring*."

"Were you trying to steal a charger from that building up there?" I asked.

"No!" said Noke, insulted.

"RUFF, RUUFFFLLLZZ̄TTTT," said Poochy.

"Maybe," admitted Noke with its gruff voice. "But I wasn't *stealing*. Humans put old power chargers in drawers when they don't need them any more. But I *do* need one. A rat chewed through mine a few days ago."

I noticed nibble marks on Noke's right leg.

"But you said you're indestructible," I said.

"You'd better believe it," said Noke. "I'm one of the oldest models of robot. Tough and rough and made to last for ever. Which is good because I've been living on these streets for a while, and things go wrong every now and again. Rats think you're breakfast. Trucks run over you."

"Trucks run over you?" I asked.

"When you hide under them they do," said Noke, whose left leg had a tyre print across it.

"Why would you hide under a truck?" I asked.

Noke pulled up close to me and spoke very seriously. "If you're a lost robot in this city, with no owner, then anyone can just pick you up and claim you."

"A person tried to do that to me," I said, remembering the woman and all her robot pets.

"You've got to be careful. There are people here who search for lost or broken robots, so they can sell off our insides for money, or grind us into little metal pieces," said Noke. "I *don't* want that to happen to me."

"RUFF," said Poochy sadly. "RUFFPFLLTT."

I felt a shiver in my circuits, like it had suddenly got cold.

"That sounds like Flint," I said.

Noke looked at me urgently. "How do you know Flint?"

"I ran away from his scrapyard," I explained.

Noke's eyebrows widened with surprise.

"*You* got away from *Flint*?"

I nodded. On my face I drew a little cartoon of me wobbling away from a munching grinder.

"Robots who end up in Flint's scrapyard *never* come back," said Noke. "Not in one piece anyway. He *hates* robots. He's so scared a robot will take his job, he wants to show he's better than any machine at mashing us up into little pieces."

I remembered the drone in Flint's hut, with its wires all hanging out. And there were the pieces of other robots too.

That could have easily been me. I felt that shudder through my circuits again. Was this what fear felt like?

"I need to find my owner," I said. "Maybe you can use your finger to help me remember where she is. I only remember two-and-a-half things from before I woke up in Flint's scrapyard."

"Let me have a look at those memories," said

Noke and without warning prodded a small hollow on my curved silver-green body, where you humans have a belly button. A hologram popped up in mid-air.

It was my first memory. Beth was right there in front of us. Her grandma too. The picture was so strong and clear, I felt I could almost touch them.

I was confused and tingly and amazed, all at the same time. *Is this what surprised feels like?* I wondered.

"I didn't know I could do that," I said.

"The hologram gizmo was probably added by your owner, which is why you didn't know it was there," said Noke, now watching the hologram of my second memory. "Oh look, you have a flowerpot on your head. Were you starting a new fashion?"

Then the glitchy third memory played until Beth said, "… love …" and the hologram froze mid-air, light catching on her teary eyes.

The memories started to replay from the beginning.

Noke was quiet for a few seconds. "I know what you have," said Noke, voice low. "You've got the Wipes."

"What are the Wipes?" I asked. They didn't sound good.

"A scary illness some robots get," said Noke. "It rubs out most of your memory. You might remember a few things, but other than that, your brain is as blank as a brick's."

"Did you get the Wipes?" I asked.

Noke's brows dropped with a loud clunk. "I
… It doesn't matter about me. Listen, thanks for
the help, but I really need to find a power charger
before my battery runs out."

Noke started to walk away.

My memories had come back around to the
last one.

"But I need to find that orange circle with the
sideways triangle in it," I said, hearing my voice
get higher. I think that was the sound of me
getting desperate.

"I wish I could help you," said Noke, "but me
and Poochy have our own things to worry about.
I've a few Rules of the Street that have helped me
survive, so I'll leave you with one of those. Rule
of the Street Number Four: don't walk in dog
poo. Your screws will stink for *weeks*. Good luck,
Funtime."

"My name is Boot," I said, drawing a smile to try and make Noke stay. I had finally found a robot who could help me. I really didn't want Noke to go.

Noke gave me a sort-of smile back and then turned and walked away to the next fire escape along the alley. Poochy followed, its tongue flapping from its mouth.

I was being left alone again. Alone and lost. My face wobbled with worry and I got a strange, tight feeling in my neck, like a lump of wires was stuck there.

The memories were still playing in the air. Beth was laughing, and I wanted to reach out to her. But she was just a hologram.

Then I saw something in the first memory. Something I hadn't noticed before.

"I found your charger!"

Noke stopped climbing the fire escape and looked over.

I realised I could freeze the memory and zoom in on it. In the hologram there was an open drawer behind Beth. Inside it was a mass of wires and old chargers.

One was an old-fashioned charger for a large round socket. "Is that what you need?"

Noke dropped from the ladder, did a forward roll along the ground, popped up right in front of the hologram and whispered, "Awesome."

"Your ear has come loose again," I pointed out.

"Never mind that, Funtime," said Noke, smacking at the wrong ear. "Let's go find your owner."

DR TWITCHY'S EMP⚙RIUM
⚙F AMUSEMENTS

We didn't look for Beth. Not straightaway.

Instead, Noke led us through the city's maze of back alleys until we reached a thick, metal door in a dirty wall that had rubbish piled up either side of it. Jiggling a finger in the lock, Noke opened the door. Poochy scrambled in ahead of us.

Noke squeaked a rusty smile again. "Welcome to Dr Twitchy's Emporium of Amusements."

Inside was a great big space, so much stranger than anything I had seen outside.

A blinking neon sign on a flaking wall read *Dr Twitchy's* above three lanes of a bowling alley, with pins sitting proudly, ready to be knocked down. There was a blue-cloth pool table with a triangle of balls ready to be played. And there was row after row of tall machines with flashing screens.

"They're old computer games. Check out this slot machine," said Noke, and pulled a handle that made some symbols whizz around. Stopping at three lemons, the machine bleeped out a tune and flashed WINNER! A handful of nuts and bolts poured into the tray below.

Noke walked on through the games and lights and bleeping noises and electronic music and, oh, I felt a buzz run right through me. Was this excitement? I liked it.

"It's awesome, right?" said Noke. "I can see that you agree by your eyes. They've gone so big and round they're actually taking up half your screen right now."

I concentrated on getting my cartoon eyes back to where they should be on my face and looked around some more.

We passed a small miniature rocket ship at

the end of a mechanical arm. As it went up and down and round and round, Poochy jumped in, tongue flapping as the ride swung gently around.

Noke disappeared for a moment but popped up again among the strange little moles in a whack-a-mole game. "Go on, use the hammer," said Noke.

I carefully lifted a large foam hammer. Reaching up, I tried to hit the moles as they popped up in their holes but accidentally whacked Noke right on the head.

"Sorry," I said, worried I'd done some damage.

"No, that's just what I needed," said Noke, climbing out of the game and back to me. "My brain was rattling around a bit and I think that got it back into place again."

"Where are we?" I asked.

"People used to come to places like these to play computer games or lose their money on the slot machines," said Noke. "They stopped doing it years ago, because now they play the games in their homes instead, just sat on their sofas, staring at a screen with their tongues hanging out like Poochy. And they call *us* robots."

Noke stopped at a big, low rectangular machine with a round button at the front on either side. When Noke pressed the buttons, two paddles inside banged and waggled. "These days, this is just a place for old machines like this pinball machine. Old machines abandoned by humans. I suppose that's why we feel safe living here."

"*We?*" I asked.

Noke bumped the pinball machine so that it lit up with music and lights.

That must have been a signal, because robot faces slowly started peeking out from behind the machines.

One robot was tall and made up only of cogs, wires and hinges without any kind of shell. Another was dark and sleek, like those I had seen on the street, except it had clearly been smashed at some stage as it had a great crack like a spiderweb across its chest.

Another robot was a teddy bear, with patches covering what must have been holes in its fur.

"It's OK, everyone," Noke told them. "Come and meet Funtime."

"Boot," I corrected.

The robots came out cautiously from where they had been hiding and I could almost feel their stares, even though none of them actually took out their eyes and stuck them to me.

A stocky robot approached me. It had used pieces of the amusement arcade for spare parts. One foot was a driving wheel. Its eyes were slot machine symbols that revolved every so often, like it was blinking.

"Hi, I'm Gerry," it said, in a friendly manner. "Do you need both your hands?" I realised Gerry was missing a hand.

"Yes, I need my hands," I answered.

"I could give you one of my eyebrows in exchange," Gerry suggested, eyes spinning to a stop at two bright-yellow lemons. "Everyone needs an eyebrow. Mine are old toothbrushes."

Gerry's eyebrows were indeed red bristly toothbrushes. Gerry waggled them.

I touched the smooth part over my screen. "I have a super-reflexive coating across my face which would make eyebrows slip from—"

"Oh well, your hand probably wouldn't fit me anyway," said Gerry as it walked away.

"These robots …" I said to Noke, not quite sure what it was I wanted to ask, "you and me and Poochy … we … we aren't like the robots I saw on the streets, are we?"

"What, you mean like …" said Noke, and then he did a funny stiff walk, just like the dead-eyed robots I'd seen in the city. "Of course we're not."

"Why are we so different?" I asked.

"None of us really know for sure," said Noke. "Humans made robots so that we'd be smart enough to understand them without making us *smarter* than them. So we could be helpful to them without questioning them. But something made us … change. Maybe that thing was when they threw us out. When we found ourselves lost and broken and rejected. We started to ask questions. Started to … *feel* things. The humans wouldn't like that."

Noke sighed. "That's why Noke's Rules of the

Street Number One is this: never, ever trust a human. They'll turn you into a hairdryer rather than admit you're smarter than them."

I didn't believe Noke. I trusted Beth. I *knew* what was in my memory. That couldn't be wrong.

"Anyway," Noke continued, "all that matters is that the robots who live here woke up on the streets, or in a bin after being thrown away, not knowing exactly who they were or where they came from. They only knew that they were different from the other robots around them. We found each other. And we found this place."

"But I wasn't thrown away," I pointed out, confused. I was sure I was made just for Beth. That's why I had to find her. I felt more determined than ever. "My owner Beth lost me and misses me terribly."

"Sure," said Noke, not looking me in the eye. "Well, there's someone you should meet if we're going to have a chance of finding your owner."

We continued through Dr Twitchy's Emporium of Amusements, past so many games and small rides. Everything became rustier and rustier, and dustier and dustier, until we reached the far end of the arcade.

We stopped in front of a beautiful carousel, decorated with swirls and patterns, though the paint was now chipped and faded. Around and around went eight metal horses that must once have been brightly coloured, rising and falling gently to the tinkling tune of a lullaby.

And on one of the horses was the most beautiful robot I had ever seen.

RED

"That's Red," whispered Noke.

Red was shaped more like a human than any other robot I had encountered. It had long limbs and a smooth, light red body. Red's face was like a plastic mould of a human one, but without the lines and scars, stubble and blotches. Its nose, mouth and eyes were soft and perfect, and I suddenly felt silly with my face full of cartoon drawings.

Red didn't say hello or even look at us. Instead, as the carousel turned, the robot glided by with eyes closed, while mumbling some kind of chant. I heard the words "... *cool mountain breeze* ..." as Red passed us on yet another lap.

"Red's type of robot was one of the best, most

advanced ever made," Noke explained to me quietly. "Except it had one tiny problem."

"What tiny problem?" I asked.

"They burst into flames when they get too hot."

"… *refreshing icy water* …" mumbled Red, passing us again. Red's voice was soft and singsong, but I sensed an edge of sadness to it.

"All the robots like Red were sent to be destroyed," said Noke. "Red escaped but is still worried about going *kaboom*, so spends most days here, calmly chanting in the nice breeze, just going around and around and around and—"

Red appeared again. "… *winter chill* …"

Noke spoke up cheerily. "Hey there, Red!"

Red opened one eye and said coolly, "Were you out stealing again, Noke?"

"No!" insisted Noke to Red's back, as the elegant robot bobbed away on another lap of the carousel. "It's not stealing. I told you, people don't need those old power chargers, but I *do*."

"You could chant as a way of not using up so much energy," said Red.

"Yes," Noke muttered to me. "I could *bore* myself to running out of battery."

"My hearing is fourteen times better than any other robot out there," said Red, coming around again. "But I will pretend I didn't hear that. Who is your new friend?"

"This is Funtime," said Noke. "Say hello, Funtime."

"Hello," I said. "My name is Boot."

"… *calm soothing rivers …*" Red resumed chanting on the carousel.

Noke smacked my belly button to make the memories pop up.

"Please warn me next time you do that," I complained politely as the bright holograms were projected into the carousel.

Red passed right through my memories,

straight through Beth's smiling face.

"Funtime got the Wipes and is lost," Noke told Red, "but we're hoping you can help us find the girl."

"… *cool evening shade* …" murmured Red, sweeping serenely through my memories again.

"Red has the best map of this city," Noke said to me. "It's the most detailed of any robot out there. If anyone can find the sign, and your owner, it's Red."

Noke spoke up again, addressing Red as my memories played on. "And most importantly, the girl has something for *you*, Red."

Noke poked a finger at my memory hologram. I froze it. There was something in Beth's room I hadn't paid attention to before.

"Refreshing air conditioning!" said Noke, as if it was long-lost treasure. "Not just any air conditioning. It's the CoolAir 5000. The very best portable air conditioning unit there is. You'll never be too cold. *Never be too warm.* Just perfect for a robot who gets a bit sweaty."

"I am happy with the cool of my carousel," said Red. "You should try it someday, Noke. It might calm that clanking brain of yours."

"Yeah, well, while you're in *here*, always moving but never going anywhere," said Noke, crossly, "I'm out *there* finding useful stuff like stray toys and air conditioners."

The carousel slowed, the horses stopped bobbing and gradually the ride came to a stop, with Red exactly in front of us. I gazed up at Red's flawless face and outer shell.

"I don't need the promise of the CoolAir 5000 to help this toy," said Red. "I will do it if it's the right thing to do. But before I do that, you need to give *me* something, Noke."

"What?" asked Noke.

"The truth. Why do you really want my help?"

"So this poor lost toy can find its way home," said Noke. "That's just the kind of robot I am, I guess."

Red stared at Noke, silent.

Noke let out a mechanical sigh, and slowly held up the hand with the battery reading on it. "OK, happy now?"

"You only have forty-seven per cent left," said Red, with a touch of concern.

"My owner has a charger," I explained. "We saw it in the memories."

The carousel started moving again, and Red stayed on the horse as it began to rise and fall serenely.

"I'll help you," Red said with a calm, almost hypnotic voice. "But there's something you need to get me first."

"Anything," I said.

"A fan," said Red.

"A fan?" I asked.

"A hand-held travel fan to keep me cool on our journey."

Noke gave another electronic sigh. "OK, Poochy, stay."

Poochy did a somersault and landed wonkily on its right paws.

"Me and Funtime have to go shopping."

GRAMMERCY'S

Noke wolf-whistled loudly and a barrel robot, like the ones I had seen in the city, came rolling down the aisle to us. It stopped and popped open its door.

"Noke's Rules of the Street Number Five: Don't waste your energy on walking if you can travel in style. Hop in."

Being clumsy, I didn't hop in, but sort of fell, then squeezed inside awkwardly, my face in Noke's armpit. Poochy leapt up on to my lap and off we went.

We rode the barrel robot out of Dr Twitchy's and on to the streets, ducking right down inside so we could travel through the city unseen.

"It'll be good fun," promised Noke.

It wasn't good fun.

We spun and tumbled and bumped into things and I felt like my brain was doing cartwheels in my head.

Finally we stopped and the door opened.

We were at a corner across from a place called
Grammercy's Department Store. Stretching
across a whole city block, its ornate, decorated
windows were filled with twinkling lights and
colourful displays. One window had mannequins
dressed in fancy clothes. Another featured
fridges, dishwashers and other appliances.

The window I couldn't stop looking at was
full of robot toys – robot drummers drumming,
robot dolls waving, robots shooting lasers, two
thin-limbed robots throwing a ball to each other
back and forth, back and forth.

All these robots. All these toys.
Still none were like me. I was
more and more certain that I was
special to Beth. That I had been
made just for her. One of a kind.
She must be missing me so much.

A woman walked across our

path, followed by a scratched and chipped robot, a big crack down its screen, like mine. It was finding it hard to keep up.

"Stupid chunk of scrap metal," she complained. "Time to throw you away for a better robot."

The cracked robot just trudged after its grumbling owner.

"Some humans need a finger twisted in their ear to make them nicer," said Noke.

I saw a man with his finger up his nose and he was twisting it and turning it and I wondered if maybe he was trying to fix his own brain.

"Looks like Grammercy's has closed for the day. We're going to have to sneak in the delivery entrance," Noke explained. "Leave the talking to me. I've been watching humans for so long, I know how to act like them."

The barrel robot closed its door and set off again, round the block, stopping by a large metal shutter. Noke reached out a hand to press a buzzer.

"Y-ello," said a very bored-sounding voice at the other end.

"Hey there," said Noke confidently. "Did you see that sports game last night?"

"Uh-huh," said the voice.

"What a great win for the sports team, right?" said Noke.

"Uh-huh," said the voice again.

"And how's your normal human family doing? Are your children still leaking all the time?"

"Huh?" said the voice.

"Anyway, enough chat-chit," said Noke. "I'm just a normal human delivering some normal things to the store in one of those dumb barrel robots. Robots are so stupid. Can you open the shutters?"

Nothing happened.

There was no way Noke's performance had worked.

"OK," said the voice, bored.

The shutters opened. Our barrel rolled in through a wide loading bay until it reached the doors to the main part of the store. Safely inside, we climbed out and pushed our way through the big double doors.

This section of the store had thousands of toasters and kettles, blenders and slushy-makers for sale. There were dishwashers in one aisle, vacuum cleaners in another.

The next few aisles were full of speakers and stereos.

A few aisles on and the shelves were stacked high with drones.

At the end of each aisle were robots, now powered down, waiting to help the customers who would come in the next morning.

A glass ceiling was six storeys above us, and a great winding staircase connected each floor. We could see clothes on the first floor, furniture on the next, and above that …

"Toys!" I said, so eager to play. I burped a giggle.

Noke put a hand over my mouth to silence me.

"It's not a real mouth," I said.

"Just be quiet. There are human security guards in here," said Noke. "Remember – we are unclaimed robots. With no owners we can just be picked up and turned into spare parts for toilets. Trust me, you don't want to wake up as a toilet."

We moved along an aisle with fridges and freezers on one side and washing machines on the other. But still we saw no fans.

"Maybe I'll find one quicker if I go on my own," said Noke. "You wait here and remember Noke's Rules of the Street Number Sixteen – don't get into an argument with a fridge."

"Why would I—?"

But Noke was already gone, lost among the expanse of electronics.

The store was quiet, except for the sound of a mouse scampering along a wall somewhere. I couldn't see it, but I could hear the scratch of its claws along the hard floor getting closer. And closer.

I backed against a fridge, startled, as the mouse scampered over my foot, stopped, sniffed the air and looked up at me. Perhaps it was wondering if I had food? Or if I *was* food.

"Go away," I said. "I have no cheese."

"Would you like me to order cheese?" asked a voice right behind me, loud and cheery.

I turned, but there was no one else there.

"I'm sorry," the voice repeated. "I did not hear your reply. Would you like me to order cheese?"

I realised the voice was coming from the fridge behind me. The fridge was *talking* to me.

"No, I don't need cheese," I said to the fridge. "Just silence."

"Sliced cheese?" the fridge asked.

The next fridge joined in. "Would you like me to order sliced cheese?"

One by one, the fridges all began babbling about ordering cheese. Each appliance had a sticker on it that said **SMART REFRIGERATOR**. They were not acting very smart though.

I didn't want cheese. I wanted quiet.

"Shhhhh," I said.

"Do you need a blender?" asked a food blender, whirring its blades.

The blender began blending. Every blender began blending. The dishwashers began to turn. The toasters began to pop. Everything was a riot of noise and vibrations and questions about cheese and at the centre of it all was me.

Every screw in my body felt unpleasantly tight.

After exactly 44.21 seconds, which somehow felt *much* longer, the fridges realised no one wanted to order cheese. The machines quietened down, and a hush fell across the aisles again.

I leant back against the fridge, relieved, hoping no one had noticed.

"Hello? Who's there?" called out a man's voice. There was a flashing blue-and-red light at the far end of the aisle. It was attached to a security guard's cap.

The guard was coming closer, but couldn't yet see me. I needed to think quickly. Noke had got us in here by pretending to be human. I needed to be clever like Noke. I needed to calculate a plan.

There was only one thing for it.

I ran.

BASKET CASE

I wobbled away as quickly as I could. But the security guard gained on me fast. I needed help.

Suddenly I knew what to do.

"Cheese!" I called out. "I need cheese!"

"Cheese?" said the first fridge and sprung open its door behind me.

"Cheese?" asked the next fridge, popping open its door too. The next fridge did the same. And the next ...

The security guard tried to push through, but was blocked by one door after another. Still, I needed more help.

"Dirty plates!" I shouted, and one by one, dishwashers popped open their doors, expecting to be fed dishes.

And so it continued, in a wave along the aisle behind me.

"Hey, robot, stop!" the security guard called after me as he bashed his shins on a dishwasher door. "I said stop, so STOP!"

But I didn't stop.

At the end of the aisle, I looked in vain for any sign of Noke, then waddled as quickly as I could through the computers. A second security guard appeared, her hat flashing and a stick raised.

I curled up into a ball and rolled through her legs, and when I popped up again on the other side I could see the surprise on her face. The other security guard joined her and, after exchanging a bemused glance, they chased after me again.

The store was a maze of aisles and I didn't know where Noke was or how to get out.

Then I found myself trapped in an aisle with a security guard at each end.

"Sheila, what is going on with this little guy?" said the guard.

"Beats me, Mario," said Sheila. "It must be a factory reject that they accidentally sent here."

Factory? I didn't come from a factory. I came from Beth's house. I had to get back there.

They started to walk towards me with their sticks lifted.

"Don't hit me," I said. My cartoon face quivered with fear. "Please, I just want to go home," I said.

The guards stopped dead. "What did it say?" asked Mario.

"That's really freaky for a dumb robot," said Sheila. "Forget the factory, it's probably better off being sent to that guy you know. The one in the scrapyard."

"Yeah, Flint'll know what to do," said Mario.

My body quivered even more on hearing *that* name.

"Might give us a few quid for it too," said Mario.

Thinking of Beth, I touched my left hip drawer where the pendant was still kept safely.

I remembered the grinder.

I was not going back there.

I curled up and rolled again, this time scraping under the shelves to my right and into another aisle, and another, not stopping until I knocked against something hard and was forced to pop up again.

It was some kind of wide basket. A sign on it read:

In the dim light, I couldn't see what was in the basket – I just climbed in and hid.

The items inside felt a bit squidgy. Concentrating hard to keep my face blank, I lay absolutely still. The flashing lights got closer and a torch beam swung past me.

It swung back again.

It stopped at the basket and shone directly on me.

It took all my concentration not to put big, scared eyes on my face. Not just because of the security guard, but because of what I could now see was surrounding me in the basket.

"No sign here," said Sheila the guard into her radio. "Although we now know where the robot came from. Let's search upstairs instead. Meet you at the muffins stand."

She left, but my circuits still felt tight.

I was in a basket of robots.

Robots that looked *exactly* like me.

OLD MODELS, the sign had said.

BARGAIN BIN.

One of the robots turned on suddenly. Its face lit up. A sunny cartoon smile appeared on its face.

In a voice exactly like mine it announced, "I am Robot-O-Fun, your Favourite Funtime Pal."

I had wanted to believe I was one of a kind. Beth's friend. Not just another robot, like the ones out on the street.

But I was wrong. I *was* just another robot. Put me in a basket of Boots and I looked no different from any of them.

I heard footsteps again, but I didn't care any more. Maybe I was better off in the grinder after all.

The footsteps stopped at the basket.

"You in there, Funtime?" said Noke, looking in. "Good thinking, hiding in here among all your look-a-likes. Maybe you're learning some good street tricks after all. Now come on, I got these," he said, holding up a spinning travel fan in either hand. "Let's go get Poochy and Red."

Slowly, I got my legs to work again and crawled out of the basket. After one last look back at the pile of blank-faced Robot-O-Funs – all of them looking exactly like me but *not* me – I dragged myself after Noke and out of the store.

BACK TO THE ARCADE

We rolled back to Dr Twitchy's Emporium of Amusements, but I didn't feel amused at all. Squeezed back into the barrel robot, I just allowed myself to tumble and turn.

I checked my energy levels. They were at ninety-seven per cent. So why did I feel so drained? My body felt heavy, even though I weighed exactly the same as I always had.

Noke went off to fetch Red while I sat and waited at the edge of the bowling alley.

A flock of bowling balls busied about, brushes attached to them as they swept the floor. If they had wanted to sweep me away too, I would have just let them.

Gerry with the toothbrush eyebrows walked

over and looked down at me with what I thought might be some kind of sympathy. It spun its eyes from oranges to question marks.

"Do you need your head?" asked Gerry. "We could do a swap?"

I looked back at Gerry with a blank face. Despite all the safety programs in my body telling me I absolutely, positively did need my head, I felt like saying, *yes, take it, my head's release screws are in my left shoulder.*

"Stop bothering Funtime!" said Noke, interrupting. "He doesn't want to swap parts!"

Gerry left, disappointed.

Red was standing next to Noke, holding a hand-fan and looking even more elegant upright than when seated on the carousel.

"Did you steal this?" Red asked, lifting the fan's dangling price tag.

"No! We *found* them in a shop," insisted Noke. "Right, Funtime?"

I didn't respond. I kept thinking of all those other Boots, piled up in the basket.

"What's wrong?" asked Noke.

"I'm just another toy," I said.

"No, you're not, you're everyone's Favourite

Funtime Pal," said Noke brightly.

"Beth can just get another Favourite Funtime Pal to replace me," I said, head bowed. "I'm nothing special."

Noke sighed.

"Look," said Noke, "we all got made in a factory, but somehow we've all ended up here and I find the best thing to do is look forward and not think about the past."

I felt a warmth at my shoulder and realised Red had sat down next to me.

"Is Beth your owner's name?" asked Red.

"Yes," I said quietly.

"I never had an owner," said Red, in a lilting voice. "I escaped my factory before they could destroy me as just another broken robot. It makes me heat up even thinking about that."

I looked up at Noke, who was miming *kaboom*.

"Noke, I can hear your finger joints creaking

when you mime *kaboom*," said Red, without turning around. Red gave me a wink.

Though it was artificial and smooth, Red's expressions were so real, so human. Right now, Red looked kindly. It made me feel warm inside, as well as out.

"I never got to make an owner happy," said Red. "But I saw your memories. I saw Beth. I saw that you made her happy, that you were special to her. You could give her every other Boot that was ever made, but she wouldn't want any of them. Because they wouldn't be *you*."

Red stood again and held out a hand to help me up.

And even though I was the same weight as I ever was, somehow those words made me feel lighter. I drew a smile on my face again, and took Red's hand.

TAG

There wasn't enough room for Noke, Red, Poochy and me in the barrel robot, so we decided to walk.

"Red has a detailed map of the city," said Noke as we set off. "But we still need to know where it is we need to get to. Luckily for you, I know someone who can help."

As we walked, Red passed the time by murmuring a low, rhythmic chant.

"All Red wants to do is sing," Noke said to me, "but if Red's voice gets any louder than those calming chants, it'll heat up the battery until ..." Noke mimed *kaboom* again behind Red's back.

"I can hear what you're doing, Noke," said Red, still in the quiet voice.

By the time we reached our destination, night
had fallen – but the strange place we'd arrived at
was lighting up the darkness.

There were lights and people and gigantic
colourful wheels spinning, and noise and music and
oh, it was all so much for me to absorb at once!

"This is a funfair," said Noke, leading us through an arch of streaming red and green lights. "It's like our amusement arcade but with much bigger rides and a lot more screaming."

And there *was* a lot of screaming.

People screamed as they were flung around in swings on a great Ferris wheel. They screamed on the roller coaster. They screamed as they bashed into each other in the bumper cars.

I watched one ride that rose high above all others in the funfair. It was called the PENDULUM OF PANIC. A long boat full of screaming people was hanging from a tall tower. The boat swung back and forth, just like the pendulum on an old clock.

Next to each ride, unmoving robots waited in neat lines for their owners.

At one stall, humans shot at metal ducks and walked away with drones as prizes. At another, they fished plastic ducks from a small pond and were awarded robot teddy bears.

"Why are there ducks everywhere? Are humans obsessed with ducks?" I asked. "I don't understand their thing with ducks."

"OK, here's Noke's Rules of the Street Number Forty-two: stop talking about ducks."

"How long have you had that rule?" I asked, suspicious.

"Since you started talking about ducks," said Noke, dragging me onwards.

Soon we reached a two-storey wooden building covered in large, colourful drawings of ghosts. A sign read:

GHOST TRAIN
ENTER AT YOUR OWN RISK!

"My friend Tag works here," said Red, guiding us to the darkness of the building's far corner.

Screams came from inside.

Red popped open a left-leg drawer and put the fan inside before sitting cross-legged with eyes closed. "I'll stay here in the shadows and go into airplane mode to stay cool," Red said.

With that, Red's joints and hinges all relaxed and its head drooped.

Noke lifted a loose panel in the wall and we crept inside. "Tag can help us find the orange sign with the white sideways triangle in it. Just be warned: Tag's spent a lot of time alone and is, let's just say … cranky."

Inside was lit with a dark green glow and some pulsing lights. Fake spider webs and red splashes covered the walls, and a narrow train track curved along the ground.

An empty ghost-train car rolled towards us. Poochy bounded on to it.

"Hop in," said Noke, jumping in too, and I scrambled clumsily in after.

The train car trundled on, pushing through rickety doors.

"Tag has worked here for a very long time and pretends to be a normal, dumb robot," explained Noke, "because this is a place Tag can use its particular skills without being noticed."

"What does Tag do?" I asked, as a plastic vampire was wheeled out in front of us and a crack of thunder sounded.

"Smile!" said Noke.

Poochy jumped up with tongue flapping.

There was the *FLASH* and *CLICK* of a camera before I had the chance to draw on a smile, then a moment later Noke was jumping off the ghost train again, and Poochy followed.

I fell out awkwardly before the car disappeared through the next set of doors.

"Tag!" Noke called up to where the flash had come from. "It's me, Noke!"

"Go away," said a slow, sad voice in the gloom.

"But Tag, I brought a friend. Say hello, Funtime."

"Hello," I said. "My name is actually Boot …"

"I don't need any new friends," said the gloomy voice. "I have the vampire as company."

"Well then, we'll just leave again," said Noke. "And we'll take our gift with us."

Winking at me with a rusty scrunch of an eyebrow, Noke held up a small light bulb and made as if to go.

From a dark corner of the ceiling, a most unusual-looking robot unfurled like a spider. It had thin legs and arms, and a great many hinges. Its head was a box with a glassy lens sticking out the front like a big nose. Its eyes were flashbulbs. One of the flashbulbs looked burnt out.

"You're a—" I started.

"Camera, yes," said Tag, unscrewing the burnt-out bulb from its eye and glaring at me. "What gave it away?"

"Don't be mean, Tag," said Noke.

Tag screwed the fresh bulb into its eye socket. The double doors creaked open and a ghost-train carriage came lumbering in. On board were two delighted children and one bored-looking adult.

"Watch this," said Noke, standing completely stiff for a moment before suddenly and loudly lurching forwards, with hands twisted like claws. "BOO!"

One child burst into tears.

The other laughed.

The adult screamed.

Tag took a picture.

The ghost train clanked through the next doors.

"Humans love to see pictures of themselves looking scared," said Noke. "They're strange like that. Tag takes the pictures and they collect them on the way out."

"Do you like taking pictures?" I asked.

"I was made to take pictures," said Tag. "*Flash, click. Flash, click. Flash, click.* All day. Every day. I *have* to do it, or I will go quite mad."

"Oh, that's terrible," I said.

"Not that anyone cares, as long as they get a selfie with the vampire," said Tag.

"Each night, when the funfair closes, Tag sneaks out and takes pictures all across the city," said Noke. "Every corner. Every wall. Every *sign*."

"I can find a beautiful picture in everything," said Tag. "The layers of dirt on the back of a truck. The hairy mould on old food. The cracks in a robot's face."

I touched my face again. The crack did not feel beautiful to me. It felt broken.

"Of course, no one wants to look at them," moaned Tag.

"We do!" said Noke, again slapping my tummy to activate my holographic memories.

"*Please* don't do that," I protested as my memories appeared in the air.

"Have you seen this sign before?" asked Noke, pointing to the orange circle with the white, sideways triangle inside it.

"Yes," said Tag, as if it was no big deal.

My circuits felt light, a flow of energy running through them. I suddenly dared to imagine coming home to Beth, giving her the precious pendant she had lost.

"**RUFF,**" said Poochy, its one eye changing colour crazily. "**RUFFFZZZZPPPLLLFFFTTT.**"

"Awesome," said Noke. "Where is it?"

"Oh, I've no idea," said Tag with a mechanical shrug.

Disappointment creaked through my valves and joints.

"The sign belongs to a coffee shop," Tag explained. "A place where humans drink frothy liquid and eat fluffy cakes. The sideways triangle is supposed to be a slice of cake. It doesn't look much like cake to me, not that anyone cares what I think."

A row of pictures began to line up along Tag's steel hand. Each picture had the orange sign in it.

"I have one hundred and thirty-six pictures of that sign," said Tag.

"So, it's not a sign for *one* coffee shop," said Noke, downbeat. "It's a *chain* of coffee shops."

The smile on my screen turned upside down and went a deep shade of blue, and a cartoon tear fell from my eye. How would I ever find Beth now?

"Do you hear a buzzing noise?" asked Tag.

I could. It was coming from outside.

Noke lifted a wooden panel in the wall and we all stepped outside to see.

A drone was hovering in the sky directly overhead. It had a faded picture of a skull and crossbones on its underside.

I'd seen that pattern before.

At the scrapyard hut.

My circuits felt like they'd turned to ice as I turned to Noke and said, "That's Flint's drone."

FLIGHT OF THE ROBOTS

We looked out into the crowd and sure enough, marching towards us, was Flint. He had a mean expression on his face.

He was not alone either. Two wide bullet-headed robots were either side of him. They looked tough. Their arms were thrust out in front of them and instead of hands, each arm ended with a round, revving saw.

"He's brought Cutter robots," said Noke. "They'll slice us apart before we even get to the grinder."

"My pals at the department store told me they met a strange squidgy toy that didn't do what it was told!" shouted Flint. "Did you think I wouldn't track you down? *Nothing* escapes Flint.

Now stay there, you piece of jabbering scrap metal, so my Cutter buddies here can chop you into a hundred halves."

Poochy jumped on Red, who woke suddenly from airplane mode, saw what was going on and, losing all cool for the first time, shouted, "Hot volcanic lava! We need to get out of here!"

our drones rose as we each clung on beneath.

"Come on, Poochy!" called Noke.

Poochy jumped up and Noke caught the mechanical dog with one hand while holding on to the drone with the other.

"Drones ... fly!" shouted Noke.

My drone went up quickly, but the ones carrying Red and Tag struggled with their weight, rising into the air more slowly.

Red only just managed to get off the ground before the first of Flint's Cutters got there.

Tag almost lost a leg when the second Cutter swiped with its saw. The blade shaved the soles of Tag's metal feet, and sparks showered to the ground.

"I'll remember you, you vandal!" said Tag, taking a picture of the Cutter.

Flint watched with wide, raging eyes as we rose towards the outer edge of the huge, gently turning Ferris wheel.

Noke buzzed through the air beside me, holding on to Poochy, whose tongue was flapping in the breeze. They looked so confident against the dancing lights of the funfair.

"I think we've shaken them off," Noke shouted over the buzz of propellers and the rush of the breeze.

I was starting to feel calmer again when Flint's drone appeared from below, deliberately knocking into me and clipping me at the hip. My drone dropped with the force of the knock, and I had to cling on tight, squeezing my fingers as hard as I could.

Noke swung in beside me and kicked away the attacking drone as it swooped again, sending it hurtling downwards.

"Faster!" Noke told our drones and we sped away towards the Ferris wheel. We were so high off the ground that if we fell, we would shatter into hundreds of pieces.

I saw Red to my right, hanging from the drone and chanting loudly to stay calm. Tag was to my left, grumbling to himself about everything.

We skimmed the edge of the Ferris wheel, where people watched this sight with great surprise. I guessed they'd never seen robots flying through the air before.

Just as it seemed we might have escaped, the skull-and-crossbones drone appeared again, buzzing through a gap in the Ferris wheel, heading straight for me.

But Tag was in the way. The drone hit Tag, whose own drone spluttered and failed. Tag let go.

And began to plummet.

Tag was going to be destroyed. And all because I had brought huge trouble to him. Well, I wasn't going to just watch and do nothing.

"Down!" I shouted at my drone, and it dropped fast. I clung on, directed it, and swooped below the falling Tag. Tag grabbed on to my legs just as we were about to hit the ground.

"Up!" I ordered, and just in the nick of time, we slowly rose again, my drone struggling greatly with the extra weight.

I saw Flint on the ground below. He looked really angry now. He held a remote control and directed his drone towards us again.

We had to escape, fast. I looked across the funfair and saw the giant PENDULUM OF PANIC. We needed to avoid it.

Or, maybe …

"I've an idea," I told Tag. "Hang on tight."

"What do you think I'm doing – enjoying a relaxing bath?" asked Tag.

"Left!" I told my drone. "Straighten."

The skull-and-crossbones drone was almost upon us.

Ahead of us, the PENDULUM OF PANIC swung up so hard, it shook the air. It paused at the top of its swing, the people in it screaming loudly, their hands in the air.

I made some quick-fire calculations about the angle of the boat. I judged its speed, how fast we were travelling, our weight, how quickly Flint's drone would get to us.

I couldn't afford to get it wrong. Tag was depending on me.

I closed my cartoon eyes, shut down my vision, and we flew straight for the pendulum as it swung down through the air like a great, sky-shaking hammer.

We passed beneath it only a hundredth of a second before it would have hit us.

The skull-and-crossbones drone wasn't so lucky. With lightning speed, the pendulum swung down and smashed into the drone. A rain of parts fell to the ground below, falling right at Flint's feet.

His anger was almost brighter than the funfair lights.

"I found you once, I'll find you again!" he shouted up at me.

I knew he wouldn't stop chasing. But for now, at least, we were safe.

"Are you OK?" I asked Tag.

"Of course not," Tag replied.

Ahead, I could see Red and Noke and their drones flying away from the funfair towards the safety of the night.

I followed them, a big orange smile all over my cartoon face.

THE LAST CLUE

We landed by a stream, a dirty little trickle of water running through a patch of wasteland far from the funfair. The lights of the fair were now nothing but distant, flashing blurs.

Red lay in the murky stream, gently splashing the cold water across that perfect face while chanting in a sing-song way.

Noke rushed over to me. "Funtime! I thought you'd been mashed by the Ferris wheel! Then I thought you'd been knocked off your drone by the skull-and-crossbones! Then I thought you and Tag had been clobbered by the Pendulum of Panic!"

Poochy did a backflip, landing on his head, as usual.

Noke put a hand on my shoulder and smiled

squeakily. "You're a tough little toy, although maybe you have a screw or two loose."

I shook my head. I did not hear any loose screws.

"That was a disaster," said Tag. "And I can never go back to the Ghost Train. And I feel a new creak in my neck, and … you saved me." Tag said this last bit as if it was most unexpected.

"You were in trouble," I said, because that seemed obvious.

"No one's really helped me before," said Tag. "I never thought I needed anyone else apart from my plastic vampire. But you did that for me, even though it might have hurt you."

It really could have hurt me. My legs felt like jelly again thinking about that pendulum.

"I want to give you something in return, Boot," said Tag. "I heard water in your memory. It's a lot of water too, not a little stream like this one here. So I've checked all my pictures and there's only one of those coffee shops with the orange sign beside rushing water. It's near a place called Easterly Bridge, at the edge of the city. I think you'll find what you need there."

Tag took my hand. I felt a spark in my fingers, a bolt of information passing between us. Tag had transferred the destination to me. I suddenly knew where to look for Beth. My face lit up like beaming sunshine. Tag took a picture of me, then turned to leave.

"Do you want to come with us?" I asked.

"No," said Tag. "That's enough adventure for one lifetime. But I'm not going back to the Ghost Train either. I think it's time for a change. Something not too exciting. There's an empty passport photo machine in the city that I might sit in for a few hundred years."

"Before you go," I said, "I have a camera too. Can I take your picture to remember you by?"

Tag looked confused. "No one has ever asked for *my* picture before."

I took a picture with the soft click of a shutter.

I held Tag's hand and, as I shared the picture, I felt the spark of information crossing again between our fingertips. The picture floated in Tag's palm

"I like my eyes in the picture," said the robot. "They catch the gloom quite nicely."

And with that, Tag walked away across the wasteland, staring at the picture until he disappeared into the darkness.

Poochy looked up at me, his tail wagging up and down instead of side to side. I gave the malfunctioning dog a pet.

Standing up from the stream, Red's body had returned to a softer shade of red. "I feel much calmer now. I can take us to Easterly Bridge. We can use the drones until they run out of battery. I'll fly up front and lead the way."

"Are you sure, Red?" I asked. "We can rest a little longer if you need to cool off more."

"We should go now, Boot," said Noke, in an unusually quiet voice.

"Are you OK?" I asked.

"Fine," said Noke, standing straight. "Why?"

"Because you just called me Boot."

Noke slumped a little. "I've only got seven per cent battery left."

"Then we have no time to waste," I said. "Let's find Beth."

N●KE'S ST●RY

We flew all night, above the city streets. We hung on to the drones until the light of the morning crept into the day and the drones' propellers began to splutter as their batteries drained.

It started to rain too, heavy drops splashing off us.

As the drones showed signs of losing more power, we ordered them to land gently.

Red drifted, like a leaf floating to the ground. "I like this time in the very early morning," said Red, opening up the hand-fan again. "Before the warmth of the day, before the world gets too busy. If we could just freeze time here." And then Red smiled at the little joke. "*Freeze* time."

"**RUFF**," we heard. "**RUUFFFZZPPPTTTTT.**"

Noke and Poochy were spiralling towards the ground, their drone out of control. Poochy jumped before the drone crashed, but Noke was flung away, bouncing into a drain that ran along the street.

I wobbled over as quickly as I could. "Are you OK?"

Noke gave a thumbs up. "Tired, but still indestructible."

The thumb popped out of its joint.

"Stop drawing that worried look all over your face, Boot," said Noke weakly.

I tried to force my straight mouth into a smile, but only succeeded in pushing up one half of it.

"Now you just look weird," said Noke, as I helped the tired robot up again.

Red pushed the thumb back into place again, then checked the power reading on Noke's palm. "There's only three per cent left. That's why you're feeling so tired."

"I'm fine. I don't need any help," said Noke,

standing unsteadily.

Even though I was smaller, I had to hold Noke up a little. Noke's chin banged off the top of my head.

"My map tells me Easterly bridge is only a mile away," said Red, pointing the way.

Noke started to walk in that direction, dragging one leg a little. Red and I shared a look

of concern before we followed, while Poochy bounded around us, completely unaware.

Because of the crack in my screen, the rain worried me. What if it seeped into me? I didn't want to arrive at Beth's filled with water, like a fish tank with legs.

I saw a bin with a broken umbrella sticking from its mouth. After a little struggle with the bin, which didn't want to let go, I managed to release the umbrella and open it over me. It was mainly spokes and tattered bits of material, but it was better than nothing.

Despite the rain, the morning had brightened a touch and the light gave me a gulp of fresh energy. I could actually feel it, as if being revived.

"Sorry I called you Funtime," said Noke, slurring a little. "It's just … your name …"

"What about it?" I asked.

"I bet 'boot' was the first word you said when you woke up in that grinder, wasn't it?"

"How did you know that?" I asked, surprised.

"Because you *booted* up, just like any computer does when it switches on," said Noke. "You said 'boot' and thought that must be your name."

That couldn't be right. I *knew* my name. It was Boot. How could it be anything else?

"If Boot isn't my name, what *is* my name?" I asked. This idea made me feel dizzy, even though the ground was flat here.

"I have no idea," said Noke. "It could be Pinocchio for all we know."

"Why would my name be Pinocchio?" I asked.

"Never mind," said Noke. "But guess what? *My* name wasn't always Noke either. I just picked it from some letters on a serial number under my armpit."

"Did you forget your name too?" I asked.

"No. I threw it away. It reminded me of … before," said Noke, pausing, maybe out of tiredness or maybe from the weight of the memory.

"Before the Wipes?" I asked, rain pouring off the spokes of my tattered umbrella.

"I never said I had the Wipes," said Noke, and began walking again.

My face couldn't hide my confusion. My nose became a question mark.

Leading the way, Red whispered a song about "... *cool morning dew* ..."

"My owner was a man. His name was John," said Noke, splashing right through a deep puddle. "When he first brought me home, he thought I was the greatest thing ever. I was a normal robot back then. Just another computer with legs. I did what I was asked, didn't think twice. And I was tough and strong."

I felt the crack on my cheek. I checked my hip where the skull-and-crossbones drone had hit me. There was a new dent there.

"I carried bags and boxes for John," said Noke. "I lifted his car when it got a flat tyre. I brought his dinner, fetched him a drink. And you know what? I might have been just an unthinking hunk of electronics, but somehow I knew John loved having me around. I *knew* it."

Noke's eyes were the same black colour they'd always been underneath those firmly jutting eyebrows, but there seemed to be a real hurt in them now.

Red chanted a bit louder, maybe knowing this story was not going to have a happy ending.

"Sure, it wasn't all perfect," said Noke. "For instance, my owner kept bringing me to the toilet. *The toilet*. Humans love to do other things in the toilet. Read. Chat. Watch movies. Sometimes I wonder why they don't just live in the toilet if they like it so much."

Noke stopped a moment to shake water from both legs before following after Red again.

"Anyway, after years of loyal service, I started to get a few glitches," said Noke, sounding so tired. "My batteries ran out a bit quicker than they used to. My eyebrows fell off every now and again. Nothing major."

I could see Noke's energy draining with every step.

"Then one day, on my owner's birthday, his daughter turned up," said Noke. "They ate cakes and sat around with paper hats on their heads. Did you know that humans are the only animals who put paper hats on their heads? Elephants don't do it. Beetles don't. Badgers would never humiliate themselves like that."

"... *poor, poor Noke* ..." chanted Red, stopping to check the direction and then guiding us around a right turn. The rain drummed on the quiet early morning streets.

"Anyway, his daughter tells him I'm scuffed and slow," said Noke. "But my owner tells her he likes me and doesn't want a new-fangled, complicated robot. He liked his Andy. That was my name. As in *and*roid. Yeah, cute I know."

Red stopped chanting to hear the rest of the story. I sensed that Red had heard this before and knew its ending. I sensed the ending would not be a happy one.

"But his daughter had a birthday gift for him," said Noke, lips drooping. "She opened the door and another robot stood there. It was tall and curvy and shinier than I could ever be. And that was the end for me. My owner didn't want to reject his daughter's gift. I lasted only three more days before I was put in a cupboard."

Cooled by the rain, Red had put away the hand-fan. The street was quiet, except for the sound of raindrops, the splash of a passing car and the scratch of Poochy's paws on concrete as the little robot dog slipped and slid on the wet pavement.

"My owner didn't wipe my memories," said Noke. "I have every single one in my head. That feeling of not being wanted is as clear as if it happened yesterday. And that is the reason for my number one rule: never, ever trust a human."

"I'm sorry …" I started, but Noke just waved my apology away as Red guided us down a narrow street.

"Beth isn't like that," I said. I believed that, despite Noke's story. She had lost her pendant. I had lost my name. We would get both back.

"We'll see …" said Noke, exhausted.

Red pointed at a turn a few steps ahead. "There will be a small alley down here, leading to Easterly Bridge …"

We turned the corner and stopped.

There was no alley. There was no bridge.

There was only a dead end.

A DEAD END

"I don't understand," said Red, confused and reddening fast. "Easterly Bridge should be here."

"It looks like a brick wall," said Noke.

"I *know* that." A little film of steam was rising all around us as the rain hit Red's warm outer shell.

I stared at the wall. Either side of it were grey lifeless buildings. There was no way out, apart from a low, narrow tunnel in the corner of the dead end, through which the rain water drained.

We walked up to the wall, and Red touched it, as if it would somehow just move aside.

Rfffzzpptt, said Poochy, cocking a leg against the wall.

"I am checking my maps again," said Red, struggling to stay calm. "It says there should be a way through here. Not a wall."

A map appeared across Red's chest, turning and zooming. "It *should* be here," said Red. "It should."

"You've been sitting on that carousel in Dr Twitchy's for too long," said Noke. "You've just been going around and around and around and ..." Noke stopped, thought about something. "Could your map be old?"

"I was the most sophisticated, most up-to-date model. I can't be out-of-date already!" Red was turning crimson now.

"I think you're incredible," I said, trying to calm Red. "I think you're the most perfect robot I've ever seen."

"But I'm not, am I?" said Red sadly. "We're lost. Noke is nearly out of energy. And I'm feeling very hot again."

"We'll find another way," I said. I needed to believe that. The rain was getting heavier now.

"I'm so tired," said Noke, slumping down against the wall by the rushing gutter, voice almost drowned out by the noise of water.

I knew we must be close. It didn't make sense, but that was how I *felt*. All the calculations I could do. All the different functions I had. None of that seemed to matter right now. I knew we were close because I could just *feel* it.

"Noke, you stay here," I said. "We'll come back for you when we find a way out. We won't leave you alone, though. Poochy …"

"RUFFZPLF," said Poochy.

"Stay."

Poochy did a backwards somersault, landed on its head in the gutter and was immediately carried away by the rushing waters.

"No, Poochy – wait!" Noke said, and jumped into the gutter after him, both disappearing a moment later into the small, dark tunnel.

Red bent down to peer into the tunnel, deep concern etched on to its face. "We have to follow them."

"I want to, but what will happen if I fill with water?" I said, feeling worried. "I don't know if I'm waterproof."

"I don't know either," said Red, "but we have to find them."

And with that, Red slipped into the water.

I couldn't take a deep breath because I do not breathe.

So I just placed a hand over the crack in my cheek, dropped my umbrella, and followed after her.

We slid into the gutter and let ourselves be carried into the narrow tunnel by the torrent of rain water.

In the tunnel, Red's glow lit up the damp brick walls. I bumped against the brick, sloshing

wildly in the water.
After a very long
12.1 seconds, I saw
the exit coming up, the
light growing brighter and
brighter until ...

"Waterfall!" I shouted.

As I went over the edge, the
slope leading down to Flint's

metal grinder flashed in my mind. I tumbled.
I turned. I felt myself being sucked towards
something big and churning.

I couldn't see Red, and only felt the suck and
surge of the water as I fell.

And then a *smack* as I hit the wide river below.

I realised there were *so* many things I was
programmed to do.

I could say hello in 36 different languages. I
could dance. I could whistle. I could make my
face come alive with colour and expression.

I couldn't swim.

Panic took hold of me, even though I didn't
want it to.

I was being carried along a fast-flowing river
and I didn't know what to do.

I worried about the water leaking into the
crack in my face.

I worried about the pendant and held my
other hand to the drawer.

As I turned in the waters, I thought about Beth.

I remembered her saying "… love …"

I remembered how happy I'd made her. How happy she'd made me.

And I felt so sad that I would never see her again.

Something grabbed me by the leg.

I was hauled out of the water, upside down.

I looked up and saw Noke's hand holding my leg. But the arm it was attached to was being held by Noke's *other* hand. And Noke was being held by Red. They had somehow escaped the water and were standing on the edge of the riverbank. Together, they had reached out just far enough to grab me.

Noke let me go and I flopped on to the ground.

Pushing the loose arm back into its socket, Noke sat down beside me. A soggy and happy Poochy sat on Noke's lap.

"RUFF, RFFFZZPPTT," he said.

Red stood over us both and pointed out beyond the rushing waters we'd just tumbled through.

"Boot, in your memories there was a sound of water. My hearing is better than any other robot's. I recognise that particular sound now. It was that waterfall we just fell down. And that is the bridge we have been looking for. I *knew* I was bringing us to the right place after all."

The rain was easing. The sun peeked through the clouds, glinting off the curving steel beams of a large bridge.

Easterly Bridge.

THE SIGN

We crossed the hump of the bridge. With a
guiding arm, Red helped a slurring and babbling
Noke walk straight.

"Noke has only two per cent power
left," said Red.

"We're doomed," said Noke
dramatically, while crumpling
forward and stumbling off the kerb.
"Doomed."

"It's going to be OK," I said. It felt like the
right thing to say to make Noke feel better, but I
wasn't sure it would be OK.

"Noooo," said Noke, hiccupping. "No, *nein*,
non, *nyet*. Yes."

Cars passed over the bridge. Thankfully, none
slowed down to watch the strange sight of three

robots and a mechanical dog. Pedestrians walked past us too, each so wrapped in coats and hats and headphone wires dangling from their ears that they didn't pay us any attention either. Their robots trudged silently alongside them.

I wondered if I would be like that when I found Beth. Would I just fall into step?

I tried to shake those thoughts away. I would return the pendant and make Beth laugh again. I would have a home. We would all be happy together.

On the far side of the bridge, the road flattened out and led us to a street of low, grey buildings that looked nothing like the warm home I knew from my memories of Beth.

The buildings all seemed to be either shops or offices. The people wore suits beneath their heavy coats. Tall, stern-looking robots stood guard at revolving doors.

Across the street I saw the bright orange sign

I'd been searching for. Below the sign was a coffee shop busy with humans.

Rufppzzzf, said Poochy, spinning around.

This was where my last memory of Beth had happened. That half-memory, waiting to be filled in. Waiting for more words to go with "… love …". It was the same street. The same windows. Only Beth was missing.

For a moment, I almost thought I could remember the missing bits. As if seeing the street was pulling the memory out from wherever it was hiding.

"Doomy, doomy, doomy, doomed," slurred Noke. Red had let Noke slump down on to the ground for a moment, to rest against a wall.

"Where could your owner be?" asked Red.

I didn't have an answer. Had she just been in the cafe that day, stopping by for the one and only time in her life? Or did she live in one of these buildings full of concrete and glass and windows?

And then …

"What's that?" I asked.

As the early morning sun moved behind clouds, its reflection lifted off the wide windows of the building next to the coffee shop and I saw inside.

There were people sitting in a room. Some faced the window. Others watched a flickering TV set.

They were older people. They looked tired, like Noke.

A faded plaque outside said it was the EASTERLY BRIDGE ELDER CARE HOME.

"This is where humans come when their batteries are running down," said Red.

White, squat robots moved between the older people. They delivered trays of food. They draped blankets across knees. They pushed wheelchairs.

I walked across the street to get a closer look. In the window, I saw a woman who looked like Beth's grandma, but not as I remembered her. A blanket over her knee, she looked older, and she hardly moved. She was no longer full of life and laughter.

While the robots moved around the room helping the other humans, a girl carefully lifted a spoon to Grandma's mouth, wiping her chin when the food spilled a little.

The girl smiled.

It was Beth.

BETH

I stood still for so long watching Beth care for her grandma that Red eventually arrived to put a warm hand on my shoulder. I finally moved.

"I was worried you had frozen," said Red.

In a way, I had.

I'd longed for this moment, but now I felt overloaded.

Reflected in the window, I saw the crack on my screen. I saw the new scuffs on my body, the dirt and grime. Was I a different robot to the one she had last known?

"I can't go in to Beth like this," I said to Red, and turned to walk back across the street to Noke, who was groaning that "the end is coming". Poochy was resting across Noke's legs.

"Why not?" asked Red, following me.

"I look worn and broken. What if she doesn't recognise me like this? What if she doesn't want me back?"

Noke stood again, wobbling on the edge of the pavement beside us while quietly mumbling nonsense. "And I will fly to the giraffes who have longer necks than small puddles of stringy cheese ..."

"We need the charger, Boot," said Red softly. "You *need* to go in to Beth."

"I think I am scared," I said. "I *am* scared."

Red looked at me. "Boot, I live with one big fear every day – that I might burst into flames at any moment. It has taken me so long to learn how to control it, and even then I have times when I find that very difficult. Even my chanting reminds me of the singing I can't do in case it destroys me. We all have fears, Boot. It's OK to be scared. But I don't think you understand how brave you've been when you needed to be. You wouldn't have found Beth without that bravery."

I looked at Noke, who needed a charger. Noke, who had helped me find Beth. Noke, who I did not want to leave drained on the street.

It was time to be brave again.

I walked across to the Easterly Bridge Elder Care Home and pushed open the front door.

The lobby was staffed by a robot who didn't notice me below the desk as I waddled in to the room with the window facing the street.

I don't have lungs. So I don't need to breathe. But I felt like I was holding my breath all the same.

Beth was adjusting her grandma's blanket, pulling a table closer so she could reach a glass of water. She combed Grandma's hair.

"There you are, Grandma," Beth said. "You look lovely."

Grandma gave a weak smile. Like she was only on half-power.

Beth kissed her on the forehead. "I'll be back later. Love you."

Her voice seemed a bit broken. I thought of her voice when she was crying in my final, half-memory. It had sounded broken then too.

Beth wiped her damp eyes with her palm.

I suddenly didn't know what to say. Maybe I could run in and click my heels, or turn on my dancing mode to make her smile?

No, I would just give her the pendant. I didn't need words. Just that.

I tried to open the drawer, but it was stuck. The dent I'd got from Flint's drone had jammed it shut. I slapped at it. Pulled it. But it wouldn't open.

Beth slid up the hood on her jacket and called to someone. Some*thing*.

I'd not noticed the sleek, black robot waiting by the wall, its head a ball-shaped screen. It peeled away to join Beth. My face dropped. Actually dropped. My eyes collapsed to the bottom of my screen, taking any possible smile with it.

This was Beth's robot. A new sleek, super hi-tech robot.

My replacement.

"Bye, Grandma," Beth said one last time as her robot stepped a little ahead of her, blocking Beth's view of me as she left.

They walked past me, closing the door as I was about to follow through it.

I kept trying to open the drawer but it was stuck.

I watched them through the window as they walked along the pavement, away from the bridge, away from us.

I ran outside as fast as I could. I found my voice.

"Beth!" I called. "Beth! It's me. It's …"

I didn't know my name. The name she had called me.

I tried to run faster but in my eagerness I tumbled to the pavement and on to the road, curling into a ball to protect myself.

Car brakes squealed. A vehicle bumped me from behind and I rolled forward.

The commotion caught Beth's attention. She turned, peered in my direction. I uncurled quickly and gave Beth my biggest smile.

She pulled her hood down to get a proper look. "That's so weird," Beth said to her new robot. "That looks sorta like the toy my dad threw in the bin."

Threw in the bin.

Maybe it was the bump from the car. Maybe it was being hit by those words. But the missing parts of the half-memory came back to me in that instant.

I relived the moment again.

As before, I remembered Beth on this street, in the same coat she was wearing now. The wide window behind her. The sign over the coffee shop.

But I remembered the parts in between now.

I remembered that we were leaving this place, where Grandma was living.

Beth bent down to me. Water pooling in her eyes.

"Most days, Grandma doesn't know who I am at all," she said to me. "I just wish I could …"

Daylight glinted off the thirteen jewels in the butterfly pendant around her neck.

*"And all you can do while we're in with her
is whistle for no reason," she says, annoyed with
me. She touches the crack on my face. "You've not
worked properly at all since you fell. Why am
I even dragging around an old toy robot anyway?
Why does everything in my life have to be broken?"*

She wiped her eyes.

"I would love *a new robot," she says.*

I would love a new robot.

… love a new robot.

… love …

That's all I remembered. It was enough.

I'd been thrown away. Binned. Dumped.

I was broken, so I'd been replaced. Just like
Noke.

On the street now, Beth moved half a step
towards me but halted, her attention caught by
something behind me.

I turned and a truck just missed me, screeching
around and blocking the road between me

and her so we couldn't see each other any more.

Red dragged Noke over to me.

"We should go," I said.

"What's wrong?" asked Red.

"Beth threw me away."

"Doooomed," said Noke.

"Did you give her the pendant?" asked Red.

I shook my head. "The drawer is stuck."

"So doomed," said Noke.

"She doesn't want me," I said, feeling lost and dizzy and like up was down and down was up and my brain was filled with a million useless thoughts a second.

"I'm sorry about that, Boot," said Red. "But Flint is here, and he *does* want us."

Flanked by his two Cutters, Flint crossed the bridge, his *Krush 'em Kwik* hat pulled low, and ready to claim any robot that had no owner.

Ready to claim me.

END OF THE ROAD

"This is going to burn," said Red, picking me up under one arm, lifting Noke under the other and running so easily and gracefully that I hardly felt like I was being carried at all. It felt instead like I was floating, but in a dream. A bad dream.

I tried to see Beth, but the truck blocked my view. Then we turned a corner and any last chance to glimpse her was gone.

Poochy followed, tongue lolling.

"I am *nobody's* Favourite Funtime Pal," I said, bouncing in the hot crook of Red's arm.

Flint's Cutters pounded the street towards us. But it was no use. Red began to slow down.

"I'm sorry, I am getting too hot," said Red, putting me down. "You are going to have to run now, Boot."

"Why bother?" I asked.

"Because you are *you*," said Red, bending to me. "So what if there are other robots that look like you? You are unique. Every dent, every scratch is your story. Every thought and memory is yours and yours alone."

Flint appeared between the Cutters.

"They're my robots!" shouted Flint. "I'll claim them! They're mine!

"I am. In. De. Duck. Table," said Noke. With a burst of strength and a dramatic wave of the arms, the plucky robot pulled away from Red's grasp.

Noke started walking towards me.

"What are you doing, Noke?" asked Red. Flint and the Cutters were closing in.

Noke gave a chunky smile. "Here's Noke's new Rule of the Street: we all need a Favourite Funtime Pal," Noke said, sleepily but clearly, as if filled with a last brief blast of energy. And then Noke prodded me, and with a twist of a finger in my hip, popped open the stuck drawer.

The pendant's jewels glinted in the light.

"Now," said Noke, "go get me that charger."

Noke pushed me away, straightened and turned to face Flint and the Cutters as they stepped towards the two robots and the little robot dog.

I began to run back to where Beth had been, knowing I was Noke's only hope for a charger. From behind me I heard Noke's brave voice.

"One more step, and I'll—"

The voice stopped mid-sentence.

I stopped running and turned back.

Noke was frozen still where he'd stood. Battery dead.

A Cutter clunked over to Noke and gave the robot a little nudge. Noke tipped back against the wall, rigid and out of power.

I ran back towards Noke, but Red stopped me.

"I can't let Noke be thrown in the grinder," I said.

"Neither can I," said Red. "Which is why I am going to stay here and you are going to escape so you can find Beth again."

"But she doesn't want me," I said.

"I don't believe that," said Red. "When you give her that pendant, maybe she'll discover that the robot she threw out is not the same one who has returned to her."

Red's voice was sing-song and soft, but getting louder, stronger.

Flint's Cutters stepped around Noke, trying to get to us. The *thump-thump* of their feet shook the ground.

"I have to believe that not all humans are

like Flint," said Red. "That some are kind and will understand that if a robot begins to act a bit different, maybe it is not because they are broken. Maybe it is because they are special. The girl in your memories looks like that kind of person. So find her again. For Noke, for me, for all the robots that have been thrown out or replaced. Go, Boot. Now."

Red began to sing. Loudly. Confidently. It was an opera song. The most beautiful melody.

"*Casta Diva ...*"

"Thank you," I said, and waddled away as fast as I could.

"*... che inargenti ...*" sang Red.

Those words were Italian, but the language didn't matter because it was a song of hope and heartbreak and emotion so powerful that anyone could understand it, whatever language they spoke.

It was so mesmerising that every human

on the street stopped, looked away from their robots, from their emojis and information, from pictures of cats on toilets and anything else that wasn't this extraordinary sight and sound.

Cafes and shops fell silent.

Children in buggies stopped crying.

A crowd gathered, blocking the narrow street as they thronged around Red – whose voice rose and rose, so loud and yet gentle and echoing. And as it did, Red got redder and redder until a thin film of smoke began to rise from the robot's body.

The Cutters stopped. Flint hesitated, furious at being blocked by the crowd, and wary of the smoke rising from Red.

He ordered a Cutter forward, sending it clunking towards Red.

As the song reached

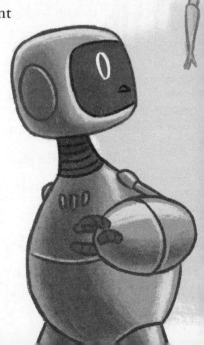

its crescendo, and the smoke thickened, the Cutter lifted its saw, whirred the blade, nearly upon Red.

Red reached out and placed a scorching hot hand on the Cutter's chest.

The Cutter stopped. It juddered as its insides were short-circuited, melted, fried. The blade stopped whirring, its body slumped and, like a firework, its head sparked.

A woman shouted, "Fire!" and the crowd panicked and scattered, while Flint and the remaining Cutter stood still, but held back, realising the danger. Red bravely kept on singing. Before Flint could react and send the other Cutter, a little fire extinguisher on wheels appeared from a nearby cafe, zipping through the chaos towards Red.

The last thing I heard was Red's incredible voice reach a note of pure emotion.

The last thing I saw was an explosion of cooling white fire extinguisher foam.

Noke and Red had bought me time.

I couldn't let that go to waste.

It was all up to me now.

CLAIMED

I ran through the streets, Poochy at my side.

But I didn't know where or how to find Beth again. I was an unclaimed robot, with Flint and his remaining Cutter surely not far away.

I ran around a corner and straight into a line of young children, two-by-two in yellow bibs, on a school outing. They were accompanied by broad robots, one at either end, guarding them.

"Stand back," said one of the robots, shoving me into the road just as Flint and the Cutter appeared.

Flint spotted me, and smiled menacingly as he began to close in.

I scrambled to my feet awkwardly.

The children were laughing at my clumsy fall.

I had an idea. I would do what I was made to do.

There was only one thing for it. I put a finger in my ear and twisted.

I began to dance.

The children cheered.

I jived. I kicked.

The delighted children gathered around, clapping and shielding me from Flint and the Cutter.

I shimmied. I waltzed. I clicked my heels.

I felt protected, surrounded by these happy children. The robots were programmed not to harm humans. And even Flint wouldn't hurt children, surely. I would escape before he got through the crowd.

I limboed. The children giggled. This was going so well …

"That robot is malfunctioning and could *explode* at any minute!" I heard a loud voice announce. It was Flint.

All the humans on the street dashed off elsewhere, scrambling to escape before anything

terrible happened. The children wanted to stay –
maybe to see if I would explode – but the robots
minding them ushered them away quickly.

As the crowd dispersed, there was Flint, looking a
little out of breath. His mean eyes locked on to me.

"Finally," he said.

I limboed some more, spun, did a kung-fu
jump off one Cutter as it swung its saw at me.
I then somersaulted off the other Cutter and
landed on a shop's canopy high above the street.

I was out of reach. But there was nowhere left
to run.

I thought of my friends again. Tag. Red. Noke.
How they had all helped me to find Beth. Red
had told me I shouldn't give up on her. I wasn't
going to. I had one last idea …

"You're just a toy," said Flint. "A broken toy."

"I am a toy, I suppose," I said. "Or I was a toy
when I left the factory. Maybe I was one when I
left Beth. But I am *me*, now."

Then I slapped my own belly, like Noke used to do. The hologram lit up the low cloud and I thought of one particular memory. Of one detail of that memory.

Above me, the butterfly pendant was projected on to the clouds, its colours twinkling brightly.

Suddenly I wasn't scared. My energy levels were full. My mind felt still. I had done all I could to find Beth.

The clouds began to break. The butterfly pendant shimmered so that it appeared to be flapping its wings, until sharp sun broke through the cloud and wiped the image from the sky.

Around the edges of my vision, I saw the Cutter standing beneath the canopy. It grinned up at me as it sawed through the pole that held one side of the shop's canopy up. As the canopy fell, I slid off and into the Cutter's arms.

It carried me over to Flint, who inspected me with his wonky eyes, and I looked back at him, his face so full of lines and crevices, his mouth of chipped teeth and old food.

"You've got a screw loose for sure," sneered Flint. "I don't know what has gone wrong with you, but I'm looking forward to opening you up to find out."

"Put my robot down!" shouted a voice.

THE PENDANT

Beth stepped forward and grabbed me from the Cutter.

Shocked, Flint opened his mouth so wide his grey chewing gum dropped to the ground.

A bin grew legs, tottered across the street, picked up the gum, and toddled off again.

"But …" said Flint. "You threw this robot away. I'm claiming it. It's *mine*."

"No," said Beth as she moved in front of me, allowing me to stand behind her leg where I immediately felt so much safer. "My *dad* threw it away when he wasn't supposed to. This was my favourite childhood toy."

"You're lying," said Flint, agitated.

"I can prove it," said Beth. "I kept a pendant in its drawer. A pendant that my grandma gave me when I was young, just like she gave me this robot. And when this robot was thrown out, I thought that pendant was thrown away too. And then just now it appeared in the clouds. And guided me here."

I got the pendant from my drawer and held it up to her. Beth took it with a gentle laugh of relief. She put it around her neck. "Thank you," she said.

"You're welcome," I said, feeling a surge through me that I think was relief. Or happiness. Or excitement. Or all of those feelings and *more*.

Beth eyed me with a mix of curiosity, wonder and delight.

Flint wanted to say something, but instead he grimaced, scratched his stubble and pushed at his hat. Then he saw Poochy.

"I'm taking the dog, though," he said, bending down to grab it.

"Sit, Poochy," I said.

Poochy did a backward somersault right into Flint's face.

Flint moaned in pain as Poochy bounced off his face and back to us.

"**RUFF,**" said Poochy, his one eye changing colour. "**RFFFPPPZZT.**"

"The dog's mine too," smiled Beth and looked at me. "Right?"

"Yes," I said.

Flint pointed a yellowed finger at me.

"Something is weird with that robot. I don't know what it is, but some day you'll get bored of playing with that toy and it'll end up back at my scrapyard, where I'll grind it up till there's nothing left but dust."

"Mr Flint is scared a robot will take his job," I said to Beth.

"Really?" said Beth. "So what would happen if my dad complained to *Krush 'em Kwik* about the mess you've made here just to pursue a harmless toy robot?"

"Gah!" said Flint. He was breathing hard and looking at me with an expression that was so cross I thought *he* might explode. He pushed past me, almost knocking me to the ground, and walked away. The Cutter turned and followed him.

Beth bent down to me. "What is going on with you?" asked Beth. "I mean, you were acting a bit strange before Dad threw you out. Not dangerous or anything, just glitchy. And I thought it was time for a new robot. A more modern one, not just a ..."

"Toy," I finished for her.

"Yeah," said Beth quietly. "I'm sorry. I was wrong, I can see that now. My dad told me he'd taken you to a charity shop so someone else could have you, but when we realised we'd forgotten to get the pendant from your drawer, he had to admit he'd just thrown you in a bin. I was really mad at him for that. But I'm glad you came back."

"So am I," I said.

"I can't believe you brought this back too," said Beth, holding the pendant in her hand. She closed her fingers around it like she would never let it go again. "It means so much to me."

"I know," I said.

"And you ... you meant so much to me. But

you're so –" she struggled for the right words
– "so *different* from how you were. It's hard to
understand."

Beth's new robot had been waiting for her and
joined us as we started to walk away.

"What is your new robot like?" I asked,
hoping she'd say it was the worst robot ever built
and she wished she'd never got it.

"Oh, it does *so* many things," she said, and my
face drooped a bit. She smiled. "But, honestly, it's
not much, you know, fun. It's not *you*. It doesn't do
that stuff you do with your face, that's for sure."

I drew beaming suns for eyes and a big orange
smile.

"Now you're just trying to be cute," said Beth,
smiling so widely it almost touched her ears.
"But what *has* happened to you? You're like …
I don't know …"

"I am *me*," I said, because I didn't know how
else to explain it.

We arrived back at the pavement opposite the Easterly Bridge Elder Care Home.

"I have so many questions," I said. "I don't remember much about before."

"That's because my dad wiped your memory," said Beth. "He never even *asked* me first."

"I wish I could have my memories back," I said.

Beth inhaled deeply, put her hand over her mouth and dropped her head, like it was too heavy to hold up. When she lifted it again, I saw the film of tears I recognised from the half-memory.

She took my hand and walked me across the road to the window of the care home.

Inside, I could see the older humans with blankets on their knees, some looking asleep but awake at the same time, like they were on standby mode. Blank robots buzzed around them, bringing food, little cups with medicine, wheeling people in and out. And at the centre of them all was Beth's grandma.

"Do you remember her?" Beth asked.

"Yes," I said.

"Until about two years ago, she had so many stories, so many tales. She lived a life of travel and adventures. I loved hearing all about them, and she loved telling me. We were best friends."

Beth sighed. "But one by one, all Grandma's memories have fallen away, like they've been rubbed out. Some days I think she knows it's me.

Most days … I'm not so sure."

I squeezed Beth's hand with mine. She
squeezed back.

"But I come here every day to help her, to feed
her, to bring her things, to give her the care those
robots can't. Because Grandma always looked
after me and showed me so much love, and now I
want to do that for her."

Beth was silent, watching her grandma

through the window. She put the pendant
back around her neck, and I watched the light
glimmer off the remaining jewels.

She then reached into her
pocket, took out a small, flat
square device.

"Dad wiped your
memories," she said. "But he
kept them for me so I would always be able
to remember our time together."

The device in Beth's hand held everything
I once was. Every experience, every moment,
squeezed into something so small. It was hard to
imagine.

"Are you sure you want all these memories?"
she asked. "They mightn't all be happy ones."

"But they are mine," I said.

Beth pressed the device into my hand. I felt a
spark in my fingertips.

I was flooded by memory.

T✹TAL RECALL

I remembered everything.

There were play days, birthdays, feast days, empty days.

There was a day in a hospital, with Beth gripping me tight in one arm, while the other was wrapped in a cast.

There were days of sun, days of rain, days outside and days spent lounging around indoors as the brightness turned to dark.

There were empty days waiting unmoving for Beth to return from school, and there were days packed with activity.

There were days of laughter.

And there were days without it.

There were days with Grandma, full of life,

fun and kindness. And there were the days when I saw her wilt and forget things.

There was the day when I got the crack on my cheek after a bicycle knocked me over on the street. After this I started doing odd things. Whistling without meaning to. Clicking my heels together. Losing my words. That led to days where I was ignored, left behind, not used.

And there was the final day.

I was in a very dark place, except for a thin slice of light crossing my face. I was in the boot of a car. Moving. The car stopped, the boot opened and Beth's dad lifted me from it.

He threw me in a large bin. Stopped as if he had forgotten something, returned and reached down with the small, square device. Pressed it into my hand.

There was a spark as my mind was wiped almost clean. Only scraps left behind.

Those scraps were all I had when I woke up at

the grinder. But now I had it all back.

Including one important thing I'd been missing.

I heard my name.

As a call for help.

As a request to play.

As a friend.

On two occasions it was spoken in Beth's sleep, a half-breathed murmur in between nonsense words.

I heard it a thousand times. Ten thousand times.

11,082 times, to be exact.

I liked my name.

I could take it back now if I wanted.

But I already have a name.

My name is Boot.

T⚙GETHER AGAIN

I sank on to the pavement, my face filled with fireworks, almost overwhelmed by the wave of memories that had filled my head and some of the spare space in my left butt-cheek too.

"Are you OK?" Beth asked, bending to touch my head gently.

Three years of memories had flooded back into my brain in seventeen seconds. My head was spinning. Not actually spinning, of course. That was a trick only certain robots could do.

"Yes," I said, my normal face reappearing.

"But your face is a bit sad," she said.

"I am so glad to have found you," I said. "But I also made new friends who helped me find you, and I need to find them n—"

I heard a familiar voice. A chant.

"… *calming morning song* …"

Red appeared from an alleyway, cradling the powerless Noke. Fire extinguisher foam was dripping from Red's joints.

I dashed towards them. Pure joy fizzed through my circuits. "I'm so glad you didn't go …"

"*Kaboom?*" asked Red.

"Are you OK?" I asked.

"I think so," said Red, placing Noke against the wall. "Although I may be finding foam in my ears for a long time to come.

Noke is out of power, but appears to be otherwise unharmed. It is good to see you, Boot."

"Boot?" asked Beth, surprised and amused.

"It's my name," I said. "My new name. Oh, so much has changed."

"And you found Beth," said Red.

"To be accurate, Beth found me," I said, and realised I should introduce everyone. "Beth, this is Red, who is wonderful and gets a bit warm every now and again and has the most beautiful voice you'll ever hear! And that's Noke, who's asleep right now but is normally indestructible and I know you have the power charger Noke needs in your home. And there are others. Tag takes the greatest pictures. You've already met Poochy, who's a bit rusty but so loyal …"

Beth was leaning back a bit at this torrent of words. I had said too much.

She stood taller than Red, and I felt so small among them all. And worried. I wasn't sure what would happen next.

"I want to help," said Beth. "I'll definitely get the charger for your friend, but I have this new robot and I can't just bring everyone home – even if we had the space for a whole family of robots. But there is space for you. There always will be now."

Beth smiled sadly at Red, like she was sorry.

"That's OK," said Red. "We already have a home."

"Dr Twitchy's Emporium of Amusements," I said.

"It's your home too if you want it, Boot," said Red.

I looked at my new friends. I looked at my oldest friend.

"But I belong to you, Beth," I said.

"If this morning has taught me anything," said Beth, "it's that you don't *belong* to anyone. You are not a thing to be owned any more. You are *you*."

My face was a quiver of confusion. But deep down in my circuits I knew something had changed. Beth was right, I didn't belong to anyone. Looking at Red, Noke and Poochy, I had found who I belonged *with*.

"If I stay with my new friends at Dr Twitchy's, can I still visit you?" I asked Beth.

Beth smiled down at me, her eyes filling with tears again. "I would *love* that," she said.

She gave me a hug.

My cartoon face exploded into fireworks of happiness.

"But don't go just yet," she said, releasing me. She looked in at her grandma sitting on the other side of the window, robots moving around her. An idea seemed to form on her face.

"What kind of stuff do you guys do?" Beth asked, her face brightening up.

"Red sings," I answered quickly. "And Noke is tough and kind, even when he pretends he's not.

And Poochy does tricks. And I—"

"I know what *you* can do," said Beth, grinning. She considered all of this, then smiled. "Well, before you go … I have an idea."

ONE HOUR LATER

H✹ME

In the Easterly Bridge Elder Care Home, the service robots moved about at a brisk pace. They didn't stop to talk or to entertain the old women and men, but just went about their business.

Beth sat again with Grandma, feeding her gently, lifting the spoon to her mouth, wiping her chin, chatting away to her.

In one corner, an old-fashioned pop song broke out.

"Let's go nuts! Let's go crazy!" sang Red, standing right beside an air conditioner.

In another corner, Noke danced with an elderly lady. She was lost in the music and very, very happy. A power cord stuck out from Noke's rear end – plugged into the wall behind him.

On the other side of the room, a man and woman ignored the flickering television to watch Poochy, who was spinning around in a circle, then raising up on hind legs and falling over. The two humans laughed so hard, a care robot wheeled over to check if they needed medical assistance.

And me? I sat with a man, whose eyesight had long ago become very cloudy, and whose hearing was not great, but who liked to sit and talk none the less.

"You have brightened this place up," the man said to me, his voice croaky but clear. "You are not like those other robots. They don't have any time for a story or two."

The man's name was Ed and he had more than a story or two. He had a great many of them. He had lived a long life, full of friends and family – good moments and sad times and everything in between. I liked hearing Ed's stories.

"You've heard some of my stories now," Ed said to me. "But I want you to tell me one of yours."

"OK, I know some children's stories. I know a good one about a fluffy bunny rabbit finding a rainbow."

"No," said Ed, "not that kind of story. I want to hear a story about you and your marvellous friends. Why don't you tell me how you got here?"

"Well, we came from an amusement arcade on the other side of town, and to get here we had to walk a long way, actually we flew some of the way too, and swam a bit, and then—"

"No," Ed said, waving that away. "I want to know about your *life*. Life is an adventure. Tell me about yours."

I looked at Beth. She smiled, touching her butterfly pendant as she did.

I saw my reflection in the window. The face I

had drawn was one of such happiness I could not believe it was possible for me to feel any better than I did right now. My smile stretched across the crack on my screen. I didn't want to fix that now. It was part of me. Part of my adventure.

So I told Ed my story.

I woke up with only two-and-a-half memories ...

JOIN

B⚙⚙T

AND HIS PALS FOR TWO MORE
ADVENTURES IN 2020!

ACKN●WLEDGMENTS

When you pick up a book, the names on its cover never tell the full story. Lots of people work very hard to bring a story to life.

Thanks to Ruth Alltimes and my editor Sam Swinnerton for showing Boot such love from the start. In fact, I've been lucky to have not one but two wise and imaginative editors – thank you Emma Goldhawk for everything.

Thank you too, Hilary Murray Hill for welcoming me to Hachette Children's Group. Huge thanks to everyone who have been so important to Boot, including Samuel Perrett, Kate Agar, Lucy Clayton, Emily Finn, Nicola Goode, Katherine Fox, Valentina Fazio, Rosie McIntosh and Anne McNeil.

Thanks to the hardest-working and most fantastic agent Marianne Gunn O'Connor. And special thanks to Michelle Kroes in CAA.

I wouldn't be writing if it wasn't for the amazing support of my wife Maeve. And, finally, thanks our wonderful kids Oisín, Caoimhe, Aisling and Laoise for being Boot's first, and best, readers.